Ticket to

GW00733450

By the same author

Eventer's Dream
A Hoof in the Door

CAROLINE AKRILL

Ticket to Ride

DRAGON
Granada Publishing

For Christine and Peter, and for Kenneth,
to remind them of our
Riding School Days

Dragon Books
Granada Publishing Ltd
8 Grafton Street, London W1X 3LA

Published by Dragon Books 1984

First published by Arlington Books Ltd 1983

Copyright © Caroline Akrill 1983

ISBN 0-583-30649-7

Reproduced, printed and bound in Great Britain by
Hazell Watson & Viney Ltd,
Aylesbury, Bucks

Set in Times

Contents

1

Last Straws

It was certainly Nigella's fault. By her reasoning, if every horse lasted a further week before being shod, and the blacksmith came every nine weeks instead of every eight, the resulting five visits a year instead of six would mean an annual saving of one hundred and sixty pounds.

This, then, was the result of it. Standing on the edge of a greasy bank, exposed to the vilest of East Anglian weather, lashed by rain, buffeted by winds; hands, thighs and face aching with cold; feet totally numb, the frostbitten toes probably snapping off one by one even as I stood.

'How far is the horsebox?' I asked.

Henrietta looked at me. Her cheeks burned red. Her hair, escaped from its coil, plastered the shoulders of her sodden habit. Her eyes, raised from the front hoof of the black horse, from the thin, twisted shoe which, despite manful efforts, she had failed to remove, were overflowing with vexation.

'How far is the box?' she repeated in a distracted voice. She dropped the hoof abruptly and took the black horse by the rein. He, after a few uneasy seconds spent pawing the air in order to ascertain that his leg was still attached to him, hopped anxiously at her side, his eyes rolling and the steam rising from his shoulders, as Henrietta set off along the ridge of the bank stretching endlessly into the miserable, mud-filled horizon.

I took hold of Nelson, who had stood like a rock throughout the emergency, his one good eye straining after hounds, the water dribbling off his chin, and his saddle black like old washleather, and squelched after them. At least, I told myself, this is the last time, the *very* last time. I am leaving tomorrow.

We walked, it seemed, for ever, but finally we reached a lane, and at the end of the lane, a pub. Henrietta handed me the black horse and vanished inside. After a goodly interval she reappeared bearing two small glasses. The contents of one of them almost blew my head off. The landlord of the pub, in a green apron, watched from the doorway with some anxiety.

'I haven't paid him,' Henrietta gasped. 'I don't seem to have any cash.'

I searched my pockets without much hope and to my relief came across a pound note, folded small, and tucked away in more affluent times for such an occasion as this. I handed it to Henrietta who, without a word of acknowledgement, handed it to the landlord. This is the last pound note, I told myself, that I will ever hand to Henrietta; but it might have been that anyway, since it was the last pound note I had.

A hammer was produced, and a pair of pliers, and with the help of these we managed to remove what remained of the black horse's impoverished shoe. Barcloths were offered, saddles were rubbed, we remounted and rode on in discomfort, clopping along the flooded lanes, through villages where the thatches poured and the guttering overflowed and every passing vehicle sent up a further douche of icy water.

There will be no more of this, I told myself, I am done with hunting. I felt myself done with many things, the Fanes included. But even now, as I looked through the slanting rain at Henrietta riding ahead, at the long and beautiful hair matted to the good blue habit, cut a little tighter in the waist and fuller in the skirt than was quite proper today, I wondered if my resolution would hold when the time came and if I would be able to leave quite so easily. Yet, I *must* leave, I said to myself, there is no future for me with the Fanes.

Every joint in my body had set into a frozen ache by the time I realized, by the welter of orchestration as what shoes our horses retained rattled, clinked, and scraped on the concrete, that we had reached the sugar beet collection point where we had left the horsebox.

I struggled out of the saddle, my knees buckling under me as I hit the ground, and fumbled, agonized and blue-fingered, with straps and keepers and bandages.

We drove home with the heater on full and the windscreen

pouring with condensation, to be received by a totally unrepentant Nigella who blamed the wet, the clay, and the sticky plough for our misfortune, and actually intimated that we had done her a personal disservice by managing to lose a shoe.

'I don't suppose you thought to bring it back with you?' she enquired, as if it might have been possible to wrench out the nails, hammer it flat, and reattach it to the black horse's foot.

By calling upon reserves of self-control I didn't know I had, I managed to endure all this without comment. It doesn't matter, I consoled myself, even though I had told Nigella it was a needless indulgence to take the horses out when there were no clients to escort; even though I had gone reluctantly, for Henrietta's sake. It really doesn't matter at all, because this is the last time I will have to put up with Nigella's misguided economies and her capricious penny-pinching. From tomorrow, it will be goodbye to all that.

Henrietta and I squelched through the kitchen. There was no need to remove our boots because the Fane residence boasted no carpets to speak of. In the icy vastness of the hall, the ornate plaster ceiling was mottled and patched with damp and the cavernous stone fireplaces were heaped with the same dead ash that had lain there eighteen months ago when I had first arrived as a hopeful young stable employee.

Now I trailed after Henrietta up the dusty, bare staircase and opened the door of my cheerless bedroom. My suitcase, already half packed, lay on the faded tapestry bedcover. Outside the tall, ill-fitting windows, the rain continued to pour down and the countryside was relentlessly grey. The room, with its monstrous carved wardrobe and coffin chest, was freezing, and its single decoration, a yellowing canvas of an angry Elizabethan lady clutching an orb to her flattened chest, her bald-lidded eyes following my every movement with venomous distrust, made it even less welcoming.

In the antiquated bathroom I fought the geyser and was rewarded with three inches of tepid water in which to soak my aching bones. I sat disconsolately in the stained bathtub trying to work up a lather with a hopeless sliver of soap and I thought about my future.

Tomorrow I would be leaving the Fanes to take up my place on an all-expenses-paid eventing scholarship and in comparison with the discomforts I had endured at Havers Hall, I would be living in the lap of luxury. I imagined myself housed in a centrally-heated chalet, wallowing in a bath whose shining taps gave forth an endless supply of hot water, taking my place in a dining hall to be served with regular, properly presented meals. The thought of it momentarily banished any qualms I had about leaving the Fanes to cope with their financially precarious livery business, and as I rubbed myself dry on a balding towel, I told myself that all I had to do before I left was to wring six months' unpaid wages out of them at supper. In the light of past experience, I knew this would not be easy.

'Wages?' Nigella said innocently when I mentioned it. 'Did we agree to pay you wages? I rather thought your board and lodging and the keep of your horse covered that.'

She handed me a plate of frighteningly greasy stew concocted out of the leg of a casualty ewe deemed too good for hounds by the Midvale and Westbury Hunt and distributed as largesse to prospective puppy walkers 'for the freezer'. The Fanes didn't have a freezer.

'When I agreed to stay for the hunting season,' I reminded her, 'you agreed to keep Legend and to pay me twenty pounds a month. "Pocket money wages" you called it. I'm not asking you for a fortune, it's only five pounds a week.'

'It may not be a fortune to you,' Henrietta said in a grumpy voice, 'but it adds up to quite a lot. We're already overdrawn at the bank and there are stacks of bills to be paid.' She removed a well-chewed piece of mutton from her mouth and placed it on the side of her plate with a grimace of disgust. 'This ewe,' she said, 'must have been run over the very second before it was due to die of old age.'

'Now look here,' I said crossly, determined not to let her change the subject, 'you'll have to pay up because I'm absolutely broke. I gave you my last pound note this morning, and I can't possibly go away on a month's course without a penny in my pocket.'

Nigella carefully studied the piece of meat impaled on the end of her fork. 'I rather suspect the mutton may have been too fresh,' she decided. 'I think we should have hung it for a few days before we cooked it.'

'And *I* think we should discuss my wages,' I said firmly.

'We are discussing them,' Henrietta countered, 'it's just that it's not awfully convenient at the moment. We're a little financially embarrassed.'

I stared at her in exasperation. 'It's *never* convenient,' I said, 'and you're *always* financially embarrassed. I've put off asking for as long as I possible could, but it never gets any better, does it? People don't work for nothing,' I told her, 'they can't afford to, and besides, what's going to happen when you replace me? Whoever you get will expect to be paid a *wage*.'

There was an awkward little silence.

'So you have definitely decided, Elaine,' Nigella said, 'not to come back after the course?'

'Nigella,' I said, 'you know I won't be coming back; we discussed it. I told you weeks ago.'

'Well, yes,' she agreed, 'but I rather hoped you might change your mind.' She stared down into her stew and looked despondent. She was wearing a fearsome mohair jersey, its matted bulk filled with hayseeds, horsehairs, flakes of bran, and other, less easily indentifiable things.

'I haven't changed my mind,' I said. How could I? Even if I wanted to, how could I go on any longer like this, without any wages, without any prospects? Surely even Nigella could see that it was impossible. 'I'm going to advertise for a job in *Horse & Hound*. If you like, I'll write an advertisement for the vacancy as well and send it off at the same time.' It seemed the least I could do.

'Er . . . no,' Nigella said, 'not yet, we'd rather not.' She became suddenly very interested in her stew.

'We might not even bother to get anyone else,' Henrietta remarked in a casual tone. 'We may find we can manage on our own. After all, it isn't *that* difficult.'

Remembering the state the yard had been in when I had arrived, I was astounded by this piece of ill-founded optim-

11

ism. I turned to Henrietta, determined to make her retract it. 'You seemed to find it difficult enough before I came,' I snapped, 'you didn't seem to find it particularly easy to manage then.'

'What Henrietta actually means,' Nigella said in a conciliatory tone, 'is that we probably won't be looking for a replacement right away. We'll keep the job open for you in case you want to come back.'

'That's very nice of you,' I said, 'but unnecessary.'

'After all,' she continued, 'you don't know what the course is going to be like. You might hate it. You might be homesick.'

I wondered how she could possibly imagine that anyone could be homesick for a place like Havers Hall. I couldn't think of a single person who would want to live in it. Only the Fanes appeared not to notice its appalling discomforts; the Fanes and the rats, who scuttled nightly in the rafters above my head. Nevertheless, I was touched to think that they wanted to keep my job open in case I was unhappy on the course, even though they would be greatly inconvenienced by it. I opened my mouth to insist that they find a replacement at once, but was interrupted by Lady Jennifer, who darted into the kitchen clad in ancient tweed and a crumpled Burberry, trailing a faded Hermes scarf with a darn in it, and looking anguished.

'Elaine,' she shrilled, 'I'm so *frightfully* sorry not to be present on your last evening, but I was *hopelessly* delayed with the Meals-on-Wheels, and I'm already *desperately* late for the Village Amenities Committee. I shall have to fly this *very* second.'

'It doesn't matter,' I said, 'honestly, I didn't expect it.' I had grown very attached to Lady Jennifer and I knew I was going to miss her a lot. Now she fled across the kitchen towards her latest good cause, pausing only to grip my shoulder affectionately with her bony fingers.

'You've been the most *marvellous* help to us, Elaine,' she trilled, 'a tower of strength. I can't imagine how we shall *possibly* manage to survive without you. I feel sure the new girl won't fit in *nearly* as well.' She knotted the headscarf under her pointed chin and made for the back door with her mackintosh flying out behind her. The door banged shut.

I turned back to the Fanes in disbelief. Nigella gave her fullest attention to her plate, but Henrietta met my eyes warily.

'New girl?' I said.

Henrietta shrugged. 'Oh,' she said vaguely, 'Mummy means whichever new girl we end up with, I suppose.'

It was a lie and I knew it. 'You've got a replacement for me already,' I said accusingly, 'you couldn't even wait until I was off the premises!'

Nigella sighed. She put down her fork. By this time everyone's stew was cold and beastly. 'Elaine,' she said, 'we had to do *something*.'

'But only a minute ago you said you would keep my job open for me in case I wanted to come back,' I said incredulously. 'You knew all the time that you had a replacement waiting!'

'We didn't want to mention it,' Nigella said, 'in case you were offended.'

'Well, I am offended,' I said, 'I'm very offended. I've never been so offended in my life, and I think you've been incredibly underhand about it!'

'What did you expect us to do?' Henrietta demanded angrily. 'Wait for you to make up your mind and then be left without anyone? Because we *would* have been left without anyone, wouldn't we? Since you have had your scholarship course to look forward to, you haven't cared what happens to us!'

I stared at her, shocked. 'I *do* care,' I said, 'I don't know how you can suggest such a thing.'

'If you cared,' Henrietta blazed, 'you would be coming back after the course, Elaine, but you decided not to. And now you're jealous because we've found someone to take your place – that's how much *you* care!'

I stared down at the lumps of mutton rising out of the glistening white globules of congealed fat on my plate. It was true. I *was* jealous. I hated the thought of someone

13

replacing me, someone else doing all the things that I had done, getting to know and love the horses that I had known.

'Elaine,' Nigella said cautiously, 'it isn't that we wanted to replace you. We *had* to. It was your choice, after all, to stay or to leave.'

I could hardly deny it. 'But you could have told me,' I said, 'we could have discussed it together. You didn't have to be so secretive about it.'

'She seems a good sort, anyway,' Henrietta said in a hearty voice. 'She's got some good ideas – she's going to take summer grass liveries and give riding lessons to the locals.'

'But I told you to do that,' I objected, 'I thought of it ages ago. I made all sorts of suggestions.'

'Oh yes,' Henrietta said in a peevish tone, 'you made *suggestions* . . .'

'We had lots of replies to our advertisement,' Nigella said quickly, 'fifteen altogether.'

No wonder she hadn't wanted me to write one out. 'If you wouldn't mind,' I said, 'I would rather not hear about it.'

'We interviewed them last week,' Henrietta said smugly, 'the day you were out with Nick Forster.'

'And I suppose you promised them a regular wage,' I said, 'even though you haven't paid me for the last six months.'

'You needn't worry about your wages, Elaine,' Nigella assured me, 'honestly. We'll bring them to the training centre when we come to see you. It isn't as if you won't see us again; we'll still be keeping in touch.'

This was the first I had heard of it. 'Will we?' I asked, surprised.

'You don't think we would just abandon you?' She dipped a crust of bread gingerly into the fatty gravy on her plate. 'Not after all we have been through together?'

'And anyway,' Henrietta said sharply, 'there's Legend to consider. We still have an interest in him.'

I didn't like the sound of this. 'An interest?' I said.

'Well, yes,' Nigella said, chewing at the soggy crust, 'of course.'

14

'When you say interest,' I said carefully, 'do you mean an interest as in personal interest? What exactly,' I asked them, 'do you mean by interest?'

'Why, personal interest,' Nigella said, 'naturally.'

'And financial interest,' Henrietta said. 'After all, we found the horse in the first place, and I paid for him out of my own pocket.'

'Now WAIT a minute!' I shouted. The legs of my chair squawked a protest as I started away from the table, confounded by this new piece of treachery. 'You may have bought the horse to start with, but I paid you back in full – the horse is now *my* property!'

There was silence. Then: 'It wasn't quite as simple as that, Elaine,' Nigella said in an uncomfortable voice, 'it was a very complicated arrangement.'

'It wasn't complicated at all,' I said heatedly. 'You bought Legend for sixteen hundred pounds, you also gave me what you considered to be a totally useless and danger-ous horse in lieu of the wages you promised to pay me and never did. I sold the horse for two thousand pounds, and I paid you back the whole amount, including four hundred pounds in interest. Legend is mine. There's nothing com-plicated about it at all, it's perfectly simple.'

'Ah,' Henrietta said on a little note of triumph, 'but you are forgetting an important little consideration known as potential.'

'Whose potential?' I demanded.

'We bought an unschooled, untried, green horse, who bucked off everyone who tried him,' Henrietta said. 'He was just about worth what we paid for him. But, after we had disciplined him, got him fit, and schooled him up to competition standard, he was worth far more; double the price at least, possibly even treble.' She helped herself to some more gravy from the stewpot, extracted a long hair from the second spoonful, and laid it pointedly beside Nigella's plate.

'After *you* schooled him!' I exploded. 'Henrietta, *I* schooled him, *I* disciplined him, *I* got him fit and up to competition standard. *You* hardly ever placed your foot in

15

his stirrup, apart from one occasion when I had a sprained wrist. Even then,' I added with angry satisfaction, 'he bucked you off.'

'But you must admit that we helped,' Nigella said. 'You couldn't have done it on your own. We helped to raise the funds for his training, we helped to buy the saddlery, we organized the transport, we even helped to get you the scholarship. Do admit, Elaine, that you couldn't have done any of it without us.'

I didn't want to admit it. I stared down at my horrible, untouched dish of casualty mutton stew, and I burned with fury. I had never imagined that the Fanes would claim a financial interest in my horse; an interest they knew I would never be able to repay; an interest which would bind and obligate me to them forever. If it was true, if they *were* still entitled to a share in Legend, I would never be free to pursue my eventing career, I would never be able to make any decision without consulting them first. I closed my eyes with despair and wondered how I would find the strength to endure it.

'I don't know why you're making such a fuss,' Henrietta commented, leaning across the table and spearing a wizened roast potato on her fork. 'It isn't as if we're actually asking you for the money.' She flipped back a tress of hair that had trailed through her gravy. 'It isn't as if we're being unreasonable.'

'We've looked in *Horse & Hound*,' Nigella said, 'and you can't get anything anywhere near Legend's standard for under ten thousand pounds. It's true, Elaine, honestly.'

I knew it was true. 'But what about me?' I asked bitterly. 'I've done my part. I've kept my side of the bargain. I've organized your yard, I've increased your business, I've looked after your horses, I've found you new livery clients. I haven't been paid for any of it.'

'Well, *that* isn't true,' Henrietta exclaimed in an outraged voice. 'We gave you a horse, we bought you Legend, we've helped with his training and saddlery, we've kept him for nothing, you've had free board and lodging yourself, *and* it seems that now you're to be paid five pounds a week backdated to last autumn. If you ask me, you've done jolly well out of us!'

'But five pounds a week isn't anywhere near a proper wage for a trained and qualified groom,' I said despairingly. 'Even with board and lodging and keep of a horse thrown in, it's pathetic!'

'In case you haven't noticed,' Henrietta flared, 'we're not exactly well off ourselves.'

'And anyway,' Nigella said in a wounded tone, 'you've been treated just like one of the family.'

There was nothing I could say to this. I slumped back in my chair, defeated. It was pointless to argue any further. I stared up at the cobwebby iron chandelier above my head. Only two of its lights burned now out of twelve. When I had first arrived there had been six, then five, then four, then three; and now there were only two. After I have gone, I thought, there will be one, and finally none at all. Then perhaps someone will buy new bulbs, and then again, perhaps they won't. Somehow, and in spite of everything that had gone before, this gave my heart a little twist and I was forced to turn my attention back to the table. I put a piece of cold mutton into my mouth and chewed, and chewed, and chewed. It was not at all pleasant, but it gave me something else to think about.

2

No Fond Farewell

There was all of a sudden a crashing of hooves and, with a lot of flying manes and flapping New Zealand rugs, the Fanes dashed under the clock arch carried along by the horses who had spent the morning turned out in the park.

With Legend bandaged and boxed and my suitcase already on the front seat of the horsebox, I had steeled myself for this final confrontation. 'Henrietta,' I said, 'what about my wages?'

Henrietta, poised to make the descent from the black horse's wither, set like a knife upon the end of his snaking neck, frowned. She wore an out-at-the-elbow sweat shirt and some ghastly striped purple, black and orange skin-tight trousers, the ensemble finished off with leg-warmers made furry with horsehairs, baseball boots and a filthy scarlet hunt waistcoat. It was not an outfit to inspire confidence within the breast of a prospective livery client, but then, who knew when or if there would ever be more.

'You must give me something,' I said, 'even a few pounds would do.'

Henrietta might have made a reply to this, had there not been a diversion as the bad-tempered chestnut, noticing that an opportunity had presented itself due to Henrietta's momentary inattention, nipped the black horse sharply on its flank.

The black horse shot forward as if propelled from a cannon, and Henrietta, true to a lifetime's instinct never to loose the reins whatever the contingency, was towed backwards over his rump on the halter ropes of Nelson and the chestnut which were clasped in either hand. She landed on the cobblestones with a thud and a gasp, finally loosing the ropes at the moment of impact with the unexpected shock of it all.

Any further demands for my wages were cut off at this

point and I could do nothing but stand speechless, as Nelson, the halter pulled completely from his threadbare little head, trotted unerringly into his own stable, and the black horse set off at a trot round the yard, snorting like a maddened bull, and lifting up his knees like a hackney. Even so, I still had hopes that the discussion might be resumed after Henrietta had struggled to her feet, looking fit to burst into flames, and I had come to and captured the black horse by his bobbing halter rope. It might have been, were it not for the fact that the bad-tempered chestnut suddenly spotted the grey cob livery.

The bad-tempered chestnut loathed and detested all of his fellow equines, but for some reason the grey cob was the horse he hated most of all. He bared his long, yellow teeth, flattened his ears, and flew at him with his tail whipping round like a windmill. The grey cob, fearing for his life, reared up against the onslaught and struck out with a front leg, emitting at the same time a shrill squeal of fright. The bay mare next to him, on whom Nigella had been sitting with a thunderstruck expression on her face, ran backwards in anguish, causing the rope of the chestnut pony on the other side to be snatched out of Nigella's hand. The pony, displaying true native instinct for self-preservation, immediately bolted off back through the clock arch, splattering the walls with gravel as her flying hooves hit the drive. It was at this point that Nick Forster, who was waiting to drive me to the training centre, set up a constant and impatient toot-tooting upon the horn.

It seemed futile to ask again for my wages as Henrietta sped off after the chestnut pony with her auburn hair streaming out behind her, and Nigella fought to keep apart the bad-tempered chestnut and the grey cob. Resignedly, I bolted the black horse into his stable and did the same with the bay mare before running for the horsebox.

'There isn't much petrol in the tank,' Nigella shouted after me. 'I don't know if I mentioned it!' Bearing in mind that I had failed to collect my wages and had not so much as a ten pence piece in my pocket, this was something of a *coup de grâce* on her part.

'You know, the Fanes have a point,' Nick said, as we negotiated the narrow, banked lanes with the petrol gauge arrow pointing ominously to red. 'They probably even have a valid case in law. Legend is twice the horse now that he was when they bought him, and you did enter into a sort of unofficial partnership to train him and provide his equipment. If you ask me, Elaine, I think you are possibly being a bit hard on the Fanes.'

'I didn't ask you,' I snapped. I was still feeling unnerved by the traumatic results of my last ditch effort to extract some money from Henrietta, and I was also nettled by the way Nick was apparently siding with the Fanes over Legend, when I had confidently expected him to be as outraged as I was. 'And I don't agree with you. After all I've done for them, I think it's crass cheek to claim a share in a horse they have already been paid for with interest, especially as, true to form, they managed to dodge the issue of my wages to the bitter end. Honestly, Nick, I'm hopping mad and the way I feel at the moment I hope I never see the Fanes again as long as I live.'

'If you don't, you certainly won't get your wages.' He glanced across at my angry face and grinned. An unexpected curve in the lane escaped his attention and we swerved slightly. There was a muffled clunk from the rear of the box.

'Oh, do take care,' I said crossly. 'I don't want to arrive with a lame horse.'

'If you speak to me like that,' Nick pointed out sharply, 'you'll be lucky to arrive at all.'

We drove along in silence for a while. I didn't want to fall out with Nick, especially as he had taken an afternoon off from his job as first whipper-in to the hunt in order to drive me to the training centre.

I stared out of the window at the familiar Suffolk landscape. Drilling had already begun in the wide brown acres stretching out to meet the sombre darkness of the pine forests, and beyond, where the soil grew lighter and conifer gave out on to gorse and bracken, seagulls wheeled and mewled over the choppy wastes of the North Sea, and anonymous ships inched their way across the skyline. I had learned to love this county; becoming accustomed to the vastness of its skies, learned to tolerate the persistence of its winds. Now I was leaving and might possibly never see it again. I swallowed hard and turned my eyes to the road ahead.

'I'm sorry,' I managed to say eventually, 'I didn't mean to snap, but I've had such guilt feelings during the past few weeks about leaving the Fanes, and I suppose, if I allow myself to admit it, I've grown very attached to them in a way. Then, when I found out they had already found a replacement for me, and they were so difficult about Legend and I couldn't even get them to pay my wages, it was the last straw.'

'Well, you needn't worry about paying for the petrol,' Nick said. 'I'll pay, and if you feel you must, you can pay me back when the Fanes pay you.'

'Thanks,' I said gratefully, 'I appreciate it.' He might just as well have said 'when the cows come home' or 'when your boat comes in' for all the promise it held in store.

We stopped at a garage for petrol and crossed the borders of Norfolk, Cambridgeshire, and Hertfordshire. By this time my thoughts had turned from the Fanes and the county I had left behind, to what might lie ahead. I began to feel nervous and even faintly sick.

Nick looked at his watch. 'What time are you supposed to be there? Before six? We should just about make it.' He glanced at my face. 'Are you OK? You look a bit pale.'

'I'm nervous,' I told him. 'I've lived for this moment for months; I've thought of nothing else and it's kept me going all through the winter, but now,' I confessed, putting into words something I had not previously admitted to myself, 'now that I'm actually on my way, I'm really not looking forward to it at all. I wish I wasn't going. I'm terrified.'

Nick grinned.

'It's no laughing matter,' I said indignantly. 'I've actually reached the stage where I'm beginning to doubt my own ability now. Remember, Nick, that I rode an ex-Olympic event horse in the two-day event when the final selection was made for this scholarship course, and all the other candidates were riding relatively inexperienced, home-schooled, novice horses. *Anyone* could have won on Genesis, even a fool could have won on him; so what if I've been deluding myself all this time? What if I turn out to be absolutely hopeless? What then?'

He tried to look serious. 'It wasn't *just* the two-day event though, was it?' he said. 'There were preliminary rounds before that, and then you were riding Legend. You *earned* your place on this course, Elaine, you didn't get it by foul means or by accident. You were chosen; so for you to say you might be hopeless is rubbish, and you know it.'

I hoped he was right. 'But it isn't only that,' I said. 'Suppose all the other scholarship candidates are well-heeled, public-school types and suppose I just don't fit in and they despise me? And whatever would they think,' I added, struck anew with the ignominy of my situation, 'if they found out I hadn't even got enough money to pay for the petrol to get to the training centre!'

Nick drove on in silence for a while. 'When I first went to work for the hunt,' he said finally, 'one of the first things I learned was that, because of my job, I would be loathed by some people and automatically accepted by others. I could never alter that, even if I turned myself inside out trying, so after a while, I learned not to try. This course is your big chance, Elaine. It's your ticket to ride, and it's too good an opportunity to waste even a minute of it worrying about things you can't alter, things which aren't really all that important in the first place – and by the way,' he added, pulling a wry face as the horsebox began to veer across the road, 'I think we've got a puncture.'

He steered the box towards the grass verge and I was out of the cab before he had hauled up the handbrake. Sure enough, the left rear wheelrims were resting on the tarmac and the tyre was as flat as a pricked balloon. Nick pulled open the personnel door. 'There's a spare under the bunk; don't panic, I'll have it changed in a tick.' A jack and some spanners landed on the lane with a clatter. I looked at my watch, it was a quarter to six. This *would* happen now, I thought in exasperation.

A second later Nick appeared beside me, looking thunderous.

'What's the matter?' I said anxiously. 'Where's the tyre? Don't say it isn't *there*!' I stared at him, appalled.

'I don't suppose it occurred to you to check the bloody spare tyre?' he said angrily. 'Because there's a slit in it I can put my fist through!'

I thought I might die of shock. The box belonged to livery clients and I remembered the day they had arrived late at a meet because of a blown tyre. 'But Nigella was told about that!' I said. 'She was supposed to have asked the garage to collect it *months* ago!'

'Well she didn't, did she?' he said furiously. 'Or even if she did, the Fanes probably haven't paid their petrol bill so why should the garage care?'

I thought this was very likely true. 'But there must be *something* we can do,' I said. 'Can't we mend it ourselves? Can't we blow it up somehow?' I felt desperate enough to try anything, but I knew, even as I said it, that we couldn't.

Nick shot me a vengeful glance. 'You'd better resign yourself to being late,' he said. 'We shall have to find a garage.'

I looked round hopelessly. We were on a minor road, surrounded by woodland, and miles from any sign of habitation. There was not a telephone box, or even a cottage within sight. 'But *Nick*,' I cried, '*how*?'

He shrugged. 'I suggest we either start walking or settle down for a nice long wait until another vehicle happens to come along.'

'But we might walk for *miles* and not find anywhere, and there might not be another vehicle for *hours*!' I looked at my watch again in a panic. 'It's already ten minutes to six!'

Nick ran a hand through his hair and looked at me with exasperation. 'Well, what else can we do?'

I had to do something.

'Where are we?' I demanded.

'Berkshire,' he said.

'I know we're in Berkshire,' I said impatiently, 'but *where* in Berkshire?'

23

I ran for the cab, found the livery clients' map, and opened it out on the bonnet. 'We're not far from the training centre, Nick! Look, we're here.' I grabbed his jersey and pulled him closer, stabbing at the patch of woodland with my finger. 'It's about six miles. I have to get there, I'll have to ride it.'

'Don't be silly, Elaine,' he said. 'You can't possibly ride it,' he slipped an arm around my shoulders. 'Stay here with me and wait. They won't worry if you're an hour or so late, and anyway, I won't see you again for ages . . .'

I was in no mood for anything like this. I pushed him away. 'I'll call at a garage and send someone out to you. I can manage my case and Legend can wear his rug, you can drop the rest of his things off later. I *can't* be late, Nick, they may lock me out, it is Sunday, after all. They may even refuse to take me if I don't arrive on time, the chief's a stickler for discipline!'

I ran round the back of the box and pulled frantically at the ramp handles. The thought of having to go back to Havers Hall and beg the Fanes to take me back was simply terrifying. I unloaded Legend, folded his rug over his shoulders and slapped the saddle on top of it. I did up the buckles of his bridle with trembling fingers, put his headcollar over it and knotted the rope around his neck.

Nick legged me into the saddle with obvious reluctance and handed me my suitcase. 'I suppose you will remember to send someone out to find me?' he said crossly. 'You won't just leave me here to rot?' He held on to Legend's bridle as I struggled to position the suitcase on the pommel and still remain in control. Legend arched his neck and pranced over the tarmac. He hadn't a clue what it was all about, but he was ready just the same.

'I will,' I promised, 'I'll stop at the first telephone box I see, and thanks Nick, for everything.' I blew him a hasty kiss. In the circumstances it was the best I could do.

I left him standing in the lane; handsome, dark-eyed, and surly. 'Damn and blast the bloody Fanes,' he called after me, 'when or if I ever get back, I'll shoot the pair of them.'

I had to laugh. It was such a relief to be in the saddle and on my way, and to hear him curse the Fanes and know he was on my side again.

'Make sure you get my wages first!' I shouted back above the urgent rattle of Legend's hooves.

3

Miracles Cannot be Wrought

The main stable yard appeared to be deserted. I led Legend in the direction of a sign which said *Office and Reception*. He had been perfectly equal to the six mile trot, but the woollen rug and the travelling bandages had caused him to become overheated. Now his forelock was plastered to his face and a gentle steam rose from every part. Polished equine heads, busily chewing hay, popped over stable doors at the sound of his hooves. I was feeling hot and flustered myself and I was relieved that there was no one to witness our unconventional arrival. On the other hand, I was rather anxious in case I should find no one to receive us at all.

Reception was empty and locked. I knocked on the door of the office.

'Come in!' a voice barked.

I opened the door cautiously. The chief sat behind a desk heaped with papers, memo pads, carbon papers, two telephones, and a kilner jar half-full of aspirin.

'I said, come in,' he said impatiently.

'I can't,' I told him, 'I've got a horse with me.' I showed him the end of Legend's rein to prove it.

He frowned. 'You are late, Miss Elliot,' he said in a terse voice. 'You were advised to be here by six. You were all notified; everyone received a memorandum.'

This was not a promising start. 'The horsebox broke down,' I explained. 'There was a puncture and I had to ride the last bit. I'm very sorry.'

He waved me away in an irritated manner. 'Get someone to show you where to put the horse and then report back to me.'

'There isn't anybody,' I said forlornly. 'I've looked.'

The chief sighed and came out from behind the papers. He wore old-fashioned breeches with crisply-pressed wings and the most beautiful brown leather boots, so close fitting and so neat that I couldn't imagine how he had ever managed to get them past his ankles.

I backed Legend away from the door to allow him safe passage and fell in behind as he strode away down one of the endless lines of immaculate loose boxes. Legend, who was probably missing his supper, dragged behind unwillingly, scraping his toes along the concrete. The chief finally halted and threw back the bolts of a half door.

'In there,' he commanded.

I dragged Legend inside. With the sweat drying in crinkles on his shoulders, his plastered forelock, and his ears set firmly back, he had never looked more unimpressive and, disloyally, I wished he would buck up a bit and prance around in front of the chief. Instead he knocked over my suitcase as he made for the haynet.

I could see at a glance that the training centre was very hot on stable management; the loose box was spacious and spotless, the windows behind the bars sparkled, the bed was laid with banked-up sides, the manger had been freshly scrubbed and the water bucket filled to the brim. Only one thing struck a discordant note and that was the sound of music – very loud, strident music – emanating from somewhere further down the block. Obviously it struck a discordant note with the chief as well, because he looked furious.

'One moment, Miss Elliot,' he said grimly, and hurried away towards the source of the discord. After a moment's hesitation, and not wanting to miss anything, I followed hot on his heels, leaving Legend struggling to chew a mouthful of hay with his bridle on.

As the music increased to a crescendo, the chief suddenly put on a spurt and flung open a stable door in a surprise attack. Inside the stable a slight girl in a red track suit was grooming a chestnut. When she saw the chief she reached out and snapped off a cassette player which was sitting on the window-ledge.

The chief looked as though he might blow a fuse himself. 'Musical entertainment is not permitted in the stables, Miss Tintoft,' he rapped. 'This is a school of equitation, not a discothèque.'

Miss Tintoft opened her mascara-edged eyes very wide and tucked her spiky orange hair behind her ears. 'Well, I didn't know that,' she said indignantly. 'Still, I've only been here a couple of hours, I can't be expected to know everything, can I?'

'And neither,' the chief added in an enraged tone, 'are students allowed to wear coloured nail polish on these premises!'

Miss Tintoft put her purple talons behind her back and shrugged her narrow shoulders. 'I've lost my remover,' she said innocently. 'I can't find it *anywhere*.'

Even from behind I could sense that the chief didn't believe it. 'You will hear more of this tomorrow, Miss Tintoft,' he barked. 'In the meantime, I suggest you familiarize yourself with the training regulations. I feel sure you were issued with a copy.' He turned on his heel and saw me. 'Kindly attend to your horse and report to the office immediately, Miss Elliot,' he commanded.

I ran.

With Legend properly rugged and fed, and my suitcase at my feet, I sat on the edge of a wooden chair in the office. The chief looked at me sternly over the papers. In my lap I now had quite a few papers of my own. Memoranda guidelines, registration forms, rules and regulations.

'This scholarship should not be regarded as a holiday jaunt, Miss Elliot,' said the chief, 'it is *work*.' He frowned at me severely, as if he doubted I knew the meaning of the word.

'I know,' I said. 'I'm prepared to work.'

'There is no guarantee of anything at the end of the course,' he warned. 'Miracles cannot be wrought within one calendar month. True, there will be a team of four members and one reserve chosen from among you to attend the junior trial, but there will be other teams, better teams, more experienced teams, riding against you.'

'Oh, yes,' I said, 'I realize that.'

'Every member of every team will be hoping to catch the eye of the selectors, praying that they will be short-listed to represent their country at the Junior Olympics; but there is nothing, Miss Elliot, *nothing*,' he emphasized fiercely, 'to intimate that you have the remotest chance of being short-listed at all.'

'No,' I said in a suitably humbled tone, 'of course not.'

'However,' the chief continued, 'if you work hard, if you prove that you have the talent, the aptitude and the dedication; if you prove yourself entirely reliable and capable, you just might.'

'Well, yes,' I said surprised, 'I suppose I might.'

'This establishment,' said the chief, indicating with a vague gesture somewhere beyond the pile of papers, 'is the finest training centre in the country; it has the highest standards, the highest percentage of examination passes, the most highly qualified staff; it enjoys an *international* reputation.'

I nodded to let him know he was preaching to the converted.

'In order to maintain our standards, Miss Elliot,' the chief continued, fixing me with a steely eye, 'we like to choose our students with care. We do not take *anybody*, we accept only the talented, only the dedicated, we take only the cream of the cream.'

I wondered if Miss Tintoft was an example of the cream of the cream, but the chief soon left me in no doubt that she was not.

'This is the first time we have played host to the Hissey Training Scholarship for Potential Event Riders,' he said. 'It is the first time we have taken in students who have not been hand picked for suitability, therefore it is in the nature of an experiment. If there are to be further training scholarships here, then this must prove successful. I trust that you and your fellow students will do your *utmost* to make it so.' His tone indicated that from what he had observed so far this was not at all likely. 'Miss Tintoft will conduct you to your quarters,' he added. He shuffled some papers impatiently, and I got up, concluding that having been suitably chastened, I had now been dismissed.

I was outside the door when I was suddenly struck by something I had forgotten. I knocked on the door again.

'Come in!' bellowed the chief.

'I wonder if I could possibly use one of your telephones?' I asked him. 'My friend's still waiting six miles away with two punctured tyres.'

For the education of horse and rider the facilities at the training centre were impressive; even my first brief impressions confirmed that the chief had made no idle boast when he had proclaimed it the finest in the country. I followed Miss Tintoft, who said I should call her Viv, across yards where not a wisp of straw lay unswept, where the paintwork sparkled, where the gravel was raked into swirls, where pitchforks, brushes, and springboks were lined up with military precision.

'Amazing, isn't it?' Viv commented in a disparaging manner. 'Wouldn't you think they'd have better things to do than make patterns in the gravel. Typical of the chief, that is.' She walked across the next patch to show she wasn't going to be intimidated by any of it, leaving a line of footprints through the stones.

I kept my own feet on the concrete walkway. After my traumatic experiences with the Fanes and their tumbledown yard, I found the professional, meticulous efficiency of the centre very encouraging. I was sure that a month of top class instruction in such an establishment would greatly benefit my eventing career, and I was elated to think that I wouldn't have to pay for any of it. I could hardly believe my luck.

I couldn't wait to see the student accommodation, but disillusionment was literally just around the corner. Behind the immaculate yards where the horses stood knee-deep in straw, the training centre suffered an abrupt change of character. It presented a vista of ugly prefabricated buildings left over from the second world war, set amidst a landscape of mountainous, steaming muckheaps. There was a pungent smell of manure.

'Great, isn't it?' Viv said cheerfully. 'Myself, I'd prefer to sleep with the horses.'

She led me across to one of the buildings. It was grey and squat and depressing, and its name, emblazoned across the

30

lintel, was NEWCASTLE. I thought it strange that a student hostel should be named after a northern city until Viv explained: 'Duke of, not *city* of.' She pushed open the door. 'They're all named after famous riding instructors; there's a Berenger, a Fillis and a Solleysell and the newest one's called Podhajsky; it's not a memorial *I'd* care for.'

I could see what she meant because the inside of Newcastle was worse than the outside. It didn't help that we walked headlong into an argument. A small, stocky girl with blonde hair and a hostile expression was berating the other occupants in no uncertain manner. She brandished an iron saucepan and her cheeks were flushed with anger.

'I haven't come all the way from Germany to be a cook!' she shouted. 'I came here to train for eventing and nobody said anything to *me* about cooking!'

As I just happened to be the nearest, she handed me the saucepan. 'Now,' she said with angry satisfaction, '*you* can be the cook.'

I stood on the worn linoleum with my suitcase in one hand and the saucepan in the other. 'I think there must be some mistake,' I said. 'I'm not the cook, I'm a scholarship student.' The other people in the shabby little room seemed unconcerned.

'She hasn't come all the way from Germany at all,' a girl, whose lank hair flopped all over her face, said in a confiding tone. 'I know for a fact she lives in Halesowen.'

The blonde girl overheard, 'That is not the point,' she snapped. 'When I was at the Reitschule we weren't expected to cook as well as ride.'

'Not to mention washing and cleaning,' someone else said morosely.

'I wonder why she didn't stay at the Reitschule,' the floppy girl said in a low voice, 'if it was so much better there.'

The blonde girl didn't rise to this. She threw herself into a vacant armchair. The springs had gone and she hit the bottom with a muffled thud. 'Ha!' she exclaimed savagely, 'even the chairs are broken!'

I turned to Viv in dismay. 'Do we have to do eventing and

31

cookery?' I asked her. I was bewildered and felt sure that it couldn't be so. There had been no mention of cookery in any of the chief's paperwork.

'We haven't got to *learn* cookery,' Viv said in an exasperated voice, 'we've just got to do our own. It's quite normal, all the working pupils have to cook their own meals as well, it isn't as if it's only us.'

I should have known this from my own days as a working pupil, but somehow I had expected scholarship students to receive slightly better treatment. Furthermore, I hadn't expected to be housed in a nasty little prefab with damp-furred walls and a one-bar electric fire. If anything, it was almost as bad as Havers Hall. 'This is an *awful* place,' I said, 'surely they must be able to offer us better accommodation than *this*.'

Viv shrugged. She clearly considered that we were all making a fuss over nothing. 'Where did you expect to be accommodated?' she enquired. 'The Ritz?'

'The thing that makes me wild,' a tall girl with spots and a greasy fringe said in annoyed tone, 'is that the chief dishes out all these memos, but he doesn't bother to tell us we have to do our own cooking and washing. Nobody does, they just leave us to find out for ourselves. If you ask me, it's a diabolical liberty and we ought to complain.'

The blonde girl gave a scornful snort. 'Who's going to care if you do complain?' she wanted to know. 'Because you won't get any sympathy from the chief, I can tell you that. I can just imagine what *he'd* say. "This is an equestrian training centre, Miss Merryman, not a five-star hotel." – That's all the sympathy you'll get from *him*.'

In spite of the stressful circumstances I had to smile; I could so easily imagine the chief saying it.

'Now at the Reitschule,' the blonde girl went on, 'they treat their students like human beings. We had really decent accommodation with central heating, tiled shower rooms, even a self-service cafeteria, and the whole place was *spotless*.'

Already I could see that the Reitschule might become rather tedious.

'But as we're not at the Reitschule,' Viv said in a cold voice, 'I suppose we'd better sort out a work rota, otherwise some people,' she looked pointedly at the blonde girl, 'won't do a tap.' She searched through the pockets of her tracksuit and came up with a ballpoint pen. 'Has anyone got any paper?'

Everyone looked blank except the tall girl who got up and unpinned a browning points of the horse chart from the wall. She laid it face down on the stained formica table. 'Here,' she said amiably, 'write it out on this.'

Viv yanked out two tubular-framed chairs from beneath the table, pushed one in my direction, sat down on the other herself and began to rule swift freehand lines across the back of the chart.

Whilst everyone awaited the outcome of the rota, I looked around cautiously at my fellow students. I had only seen them once before and then briefly, at the two-day event where the chief had been officiating, and where the successful scholarship candidates had been finally chosen. Then, they had just been anonymous competitors and rivals, uniformly black-coated for the dressage and show-jumping, or helmeted for the cross-country. It had not actually occurred to me that they might not be well-heeled, eventing types at all, but just ordinary, run-of-the-mill people like myself, and I didn't know whether to be relieved or disappointed. But then, I reflected ruefully, well-heeled, eventing types could afford to pay for their own training, they didn't have to try for scholarships given for publicity purposes by commercial enterprise.

'I don't know how I'll manage when it's my turn to cook,' the girl with floppy hair, whose name turned out to be Mandy, said in an anxious voice. She leaned over Viv's shoulder and twisted a lump of hair nervously round a finger with the nail bitten to the quick. 'I can't even boil water, and I'll never manage the cleaning either; I've never touched a washing machine, and I had an auntie who was electrocuted by a vacuum cleaner.'

The tall girl gave a loud honk of laughter.

'You won't get electrocuted here,' Viv told her, 'unless

you're thinking of plugging in the dustpan and brush.' She got up from the table and pinned the rota on to the wall. We all gathered round to look at it.

There were seven scholarship students altogether, although only five of us had arrived so far. There seemed to be some doubt about one of the missing students as Alice, the tall girl with spots, had heard she had broken a leg out hunting, but as this couldn't be confirmed she had been added to the rota anyway in the hope that the information had been false. Over the twenty-eight days we were each allocated four days of cooking, plus one stint of washing, which meant that if we agreed to make our own beds and to make a conscious effort to keep the Duke of Newcastle tidy, we each cooked one day a week and did one shared stint of washing. Put like this it didn't sound so bad, and even Annemarie, from the Reitschule and Halesowen, had to agree that it was fair.

This being settled, and I having resigned myself to the fact that it was the instruction, not the accommodation, that was more important, I set out to explore the Duke of Newcastle.

My Ideal Home for the next four weeks was pretty squalid and a far cry from the luxurious centrally-heated chalet I had imagined. Leading off from the nasty sitting room, which doubled as a dining room, was a cramped hallway which managed to contain a further six doors. Four of these led into four identical little cells each containing two narrow divan beds separated by the sort of hateful little bedside cupboards which used to house a chamber pot. These didn't, because struck by the alarming possibility that the Duke of Newcastle might not even be blessed with indoor sanitation, I checked.

On top of the cupboards were bedside lamps made from Chianti bottles topped by fly-blown pleated paper lampshades, and the only other furnishing was a metal dress rail which presumably served as a wardrobe. All this made my bedroom at Havers Hall, with its half-tester bed, its carved wardrobe and coffin chest, positively palatial.

On the door of each cell was a notice. It said:

No smoking, alcohol, boots, food,
electric kettles or male persons
permitted in the bedrooms.

It was signed by the chief. As I continued my tour of inspection I found many more similar notices also signed by the chief. In the bathroom, with its chipped porcelain and rotting lino, there was one pasted to the hot water cupboards.

This immersion heater must NOT be
left on all night.
ELECTRICITY COSTS MONEY.

And in the dismal cubby hole that proclaimed itself the kitchen, yet another was sellotaped to the door of the refrigerator.

This refrigerator MUST be defrosted
every THREE days. Biological specimens
and worm counts are NOT to be kept in
this refrigerator, it is for foodstuffs
ONLY.

One wall of the kitchen was lined with open shelves stacked with saucepans with defective handles and odd lids. There were some piles of miscellaneous plates and mugs, and a drawer revealed a selection of assorted cutlery. In a cabinet, fronted with sliding doors of yellowing frosted glass, I found a half-empty packet of cereal, a jar of solidified Horlicks, and a vast selection of Hissey's pickles. Since Hissey's Pickle Company were sponsoring the scholarship course, this was a neat touch, but there was no sign of anything we could actually eat.

It was only when I opened the back door that I found a large carton bearing the grand inscription PROVISIONS FOR THE DUKE OF NEWCASTLE. I lifted the lid cautiously and saw a cold chicken, salad vegetables, milk, butter, bread, instant coffee and other welcome things. At least, I told myself as I carried the carton into the sitting room to show to the others, it's an improvement on the Fanes' mutton stew.

4

To Horse!

We were just breakfasting off the remains of the Duke of Newcastle's chicken, and wondering what had happened to the other scholarship students, when there was a knock at the door.

'Come in,' Alice shouted, 'we're all decent!'

The door opened to reveal a tall girl in an immaculate cream woollen suit and a fur jacket. She had glossy brown hair coiled into a neat bun, her nose was rather too long, and her eyes were set close together which had the unfortunate effect of making her look like a snooty sheep. She smiled at us brightly.

'Good morning,' she said in a superior, school-mistressy sort of voice, 'I'm Selina Gibbons.' She craned her well-groomed neck round the door in order to survey the room and the smile vanished. 'What a *frightful* place,' she said in distaste. She came inside, lifting her expensively shod feet up rather high, as if she expected to step into something unpleasant.

'Would you believe it,' Alice said in surprise, 'Selina Gibbons. I heard you'd broken a leg.'

'I can hardly have broken a leg, can I?' Selina said sweetly. 'Otherwise I wouldn't be here, would I? Otherwise my leg would be in plaster, wouldn't it?' She looked at Alice and frowned slightly. 'Ought I to know you?' she wondered, then, before Alice could open her mouth to reply: 'No,' she decided, 'I rather think not.' She peeled off the thinnest of leather gloves. 'Do you think that one of you could help me with my bags?' she said, adding, as none of us moved to do so, '*If* you would be so kind.'

Mandy jumped up and began to haul in a set of matching suitcases from the doorway. Selina was already in the hall looking for her bedroom. The rest of us exchanged stunned glances across the breakfast table. It didn't take Selina long to inspect the Duke of Newcastle but although she was clearly somewhat discomforted by what she had seen, she seemed determined to put a brave face on it. She looked disapprovingly at the litter of crusts and milk bottles on the table. 'I have breakfasted,' she informed us, recoiling slightly as she noticed the chicken carcass, 'so please don't trouble on my behalf.'

'How very fortunate,' Alice commented in a dry tone, 'because there's nothing left anyway.'

Selina favoured Alice with a tight little smile and stepped around us in order to inspect the rota. I wondered what her reaction would be when she discovered that she was expected to take her turn with the cooking and the washing but she made no comment. She seemed more interested in everyone's names.

'Vivienne Tintoft,' she exclaimed, 'not one of *the* Tintofts, surely? Not the Tintoft family who own the departmental stores?'

Viv, who had been spooning up the sugar left at the bottom of her coffee, dropped the spoon into the mug. 'Come to think of it,' she said, 'my old man is in the retail trade.'

'Really?' Selina looked round, interested.

Viv nodded. 'He's got a market stall down the Mile End Road.'

Selina wrinkled up her long nose as if she had just come into contact with a bad smell. 'A market *stall*?' she said, appalled.

'That's right,' said Viv cheerfully, 'handbags, belts, Indian sandals; you know the sort of thing.'

Selina looked pained. 'I'm not exactly sure that I do,' she said.

Annemarie, who had been listening to all this with a bored expression on her face, now looked at her watch and announced that it was ten minutes to ten. There was a sudden flurry as everyone made for their cells because we were due for a briefing from the chief in the lecture hall at ten o'clock. Somehow I had found myself sharing a cell with Annemarie, and as we jostled one another for the benefit of the tiny spotted mirror on the wall, Viv appeared looking distracted.

'I *can't* share a room with Selina Gibbons,' she groaned, 'she'll drive me barmy. She's in there now lining the drawers with tissue paper and looking for fleas in the mattress. She's even brought her own sheets and pillowcases.'

'I'll change with you, if you like,' I offered. The truth of the matter was that I didn't feel I could face four weeks of Annemarie as a bedfellow. She had snored hideously and unceasingly all through the previous night until I, sleepless and distraught, had longed to be back under the faded tapestry bedcover at Havers Hall. Yet when I had mentioned it in the morning, she had denied it so vehemently that I half-believed I had dreamed it. I knew I would never dare to bring up the subject again.

Before she could object to sharing a room with Viv, I left Annemarie sole use of the mirror and went to inform Selina that I was her new cellmate.

'Whoever shares a room with me,' she remarked, as soon as I put my nose inside the door, '*must* be tidy. I do insist upon an orderly room.' One of her smaller cases had turned itself into a typewriter. This seemed to be a surprising item of equipment to bring on a scholarship course, and Selina, following the direction of my eyes, snapped the the lid shut.

'I do have rather a lot of personal correspondence to attend to,' she said by way of explanation, '*private* correspondence,' she added, as if she suspected I might be the kind of person who had a penchant for reading other people's letters. I withdrew.

We all arrived at the lecture hall together and sat down, taking up half of the first row of chairs. We were only five seconds ahead of the chief, who marched down the centre aisle in his gleaming boots and gave us a curt nod. He took up a position behind an ecclesiastical lecture stand and shuffled an array of papers.

'I shall not delay you long,' he said, looking at us sharply, as if we were already late for three appointments and had really no right to be sitting there at all.

'So kind,' Selina murmured. 'It does take one a little time to settle in.'

The chief stared at her as if he found her comment totally incomprehensible. 'Hand out these sheets to the rest of the students,' he rapped, 'Miss er . . .' he paused to look down his list of names.

'Gibbons,' Selina supplied. She took the proffered sheets and graciously handed one to each of us.

'Without a broken leg,' Alice commented in a low voice, '*if* you would be so kind.'

Selina gave her an icy look and sat down, folding her legs neatly under her chair like a professional model.

'Have you *seen* this?' Annemarie hissed in my ear. 'We have to be out in the yard by six o'clock, and we have to go out running for half an hour every day – *running*,' she repeated in a scandalized voice.

'Silence, if you *please*!' the chief barked. 'This is a briefing, not a ladies' coffee morning!'

Annemarie snapped upright in her chair.

'This morning,' said the chief, 'we shall begin with an assessment period in the indoor school, a break for lunch, followed by a further assessment of a restricted nature on the cross-country course. I shall be assessing capabilities, potential, and fitness, not only of yourselves, but of your horses – ' he drew a deep breath as if to signify that there might be precious little to assess, 'after which I shall draw up individual tables of exercise, work, and feeding for your horses, and set each of you appropriately timed periods of running, lunging without reins and stirrups, and riding, to produce maximum fitness and performance with a view to competing in the junior trial at the end of the month.' He looked at each of us carefully to see how we would take this. We stared back at him in silence.

'Until I have worked out your individual programmes,' he continued, 'you will kindly follow the daily schedule.'

'Which daily schedule is that?' Selina enquired sweetly.

'The daily schedule sitting on your lap,' the chief snapped.

'Oh, I see,' Selina said, undismayed, 'I do beg your pardon.'

40

Alice sniggered.

'You may now return to your quarters in order to change for the assessment lesson.' The chief stared at Alice and narrowed his eyes. Alice stared back. The chief averted his gaze hastily. 'I shall expect you to report to the indoor school in fifteen minutes precisely,' he commanded.

'I may be a little longer than that,' Selina informed him, 'I have yet to unpack.'

The chief's face took on a slightly darker hue. 'Miss Gibbons,' he said, 'I repeat, I expect to see you in the indoor school in *fifteen minutes*.'

Selina gave him a brave smile. 'Very well,' she promised, 'I shall do my best.' She got up to leave.

'Kindly remain seated until I give you permission to rise!' the chief bellowed.

Selina sat down again with a bump. Now it was her turn to look at the chief as if he might be insane. It occurred to me that he didn't appear to have had much practice in dealing with the cream of the cream.

'Rather natty, don't you think?'

Selina pulled a pair of breeches over her long, thin, elegant legs. They were cream, with velcro fastenings and soft, pale suede strapping from seat to calf, absolutely identical to the pair lying swathed in tissue in the bottom of my drawer, awaiting my first three-day event.

Resignedly, I took out my second best. Selina was already sporting a tweed coat by Weatherill, and had unpacked a pair of long riding boots which, even without looking, I knew would he handmade by Maxwell. One could never compete; it would be ridiculous to try.

'As a matter of interest,' I asked her, attempting to cram my hair into a net without the benefit of the mirror because Selina was already firmly installed in front of it, fiddling with a silky cravat, 'why did you try for a scholarship? Why didn't you just pay for your training, and do the whole thing in comfort?'

Selina stabbed at the cravat with a gold stock pin. 'Because one does rather like to feel that one has been accepted on merit,' she said in a reproving tone, 'not simply because one can foot the bill.'

We made our way past the muckheaps, their familiar sweet, sickly smell shot through with powerful whiffs of ammonia, on our way to the high-powered frenetic efficiency of the yards where staff and working pupils alike were engaged in an unceasing round of activity. People hurried up and down the walkways, carrying saddles, draped with bridles and headcollars, half-buried under mounds of coloured rugs and striped stable blankets. Horses clopped in and out, springboks flew above the gravel, wooden water pails waited in rows beside the taps, hay nets were being stuffed and weighed in the barns, leather was being soaped in the tackrooms. In the large open-fronted boxes at the end of each row, electric groomers or clippers whirred busily, and from somewhere came the distinctive acrid smell of burned horn which told of a blacksmith at work.

We had all been out early to feed and muck out our own horses, and I had strapped Legend and washed his mane and tail. He seemed to have settled in perfectly and I found him looking over the top half of his door, interested in everything that was going on, but even so, he caught my step as I approached along the walkway and turned his bay head with its white star shining, and whickered a soft welcome.

On the front of the lower door was a perspex slot into which a card had been dropped. THE HISSEY TRAINING SCHOLARSHIP it read, and underneath our names, ANOTHER LEGEND, Owner/rider ELAINE ELLIOT. There was a space under this for further information, and although mine was left blank, most of the other cards around the yard had theirs filled in. RUG TEARER one said, and then BOLTS FOOD – LARGE STONES TO BE LEFT IN MANGER, and more unwelcoming, STRIKES OUT WITH FRONT FEET. I was rather glad I couldn't think of anything to write about Legend.

The scholarship students had all been allocated boxes in the same yard. Annemarie's horse, a well-made and compact part-bred Hanoverian, bought in Germany where Annemarie's father was a British serving officer, was stabled next to Legend. 'He's small for an eventer, but he's got a lion's heart,' she told me fiercely, as we led our horses across the gravel towards the indoor school. 'He's good enough for the Junior Olympics, and I mean to get there. We haven't spent two months at the Reitschule for nothing.'

As we entered by the sliding doors, the chief was standing in the middle of the school eyeing his watch. 'One moment!' he rapped, effectively halting us in our tracks as we began to prepare to mount. 'Kindly make a line in front of me, *dis*-mounted.'

We shuffled ourselves and our horses into a line, surprised.

The chief marched up to Alice who had positioned herself at one end of the line and peered closely at her face. 'Better see the nurse,' he said curtly.

Alice was astonished. 'What for?' she demanded, as soon as she could find her voice.

'Spots,' said the chief, 'can't have a girl with spots. Unhealthy. Might be catching.'

'Rubbish,' Alice said scornfully, 'it's my age.'

The chief pointed his stick at her chest. 'Button missing,' he observed, flipping open her jacket. His eyes travelled downwards, 'boot straps upside down.' He moved on to Mandy, leaving Alice with her mouth agape.

Mandy stared at the chief like a mesmerized rabbit. She wore her hat with the peak pointing upwards and her awful floppy hair hung out all round.

'Hairnet?' the chief snapped.

Mandy jumped and grabbed nervously at her hair. 'I haven't got one,' she said.

'Obviously,' the chief said in a dry voice. 'Kindly see that you are equipped with one in future.' He reached out and pulled the peak of her hat straight. Mandy flinched. I think she actually imagined he was going to box her ears.

The chief looked Selina up and down almost approvingly. 'Very good, Miss Gibbons,' he said. Selina smiled at him in an ingratiating manner.

Annemarie was next. She stood like a ramrod with every item of her kit clean and correct and her boots shining like mirrors, but even so, the chief found something to complain about. 'Be good enough to remove your earrings, Miss Maddox,' he said sharply. 'This is a centre of equitation, not a West End nightclub.'

Beside me, Viv let out a strangled squeak of mirth. Annemarie began to fumble with her ear lobes. 'Yes sir,' she said.

It was my turn. The chief frowned and stared at my neck. I waited for him to say it was dirty, because I hadn't been able to have a proper wash all day. Every time I had tried to get into the bathroom it had been occupied by someone else. I had ended up washing just my hands and my face in the kitchen sink, over a pile of dirty dishes that nobody would accept responsibility for – the rota not being very specific about things like washingup. However, it wasn't my neck he was looking at.

'I would prefer a collar and tie to a roll-necked jersey, Miss Elliot,' he rapped. 'This is a formal lesson, not a hack in the park.'

'I'll change it,' I promised, 'before the next lesson.'

'You will indeed,' he agreed, and he passed on to Viv.

Viv's lips were pressed together and her cheeks were pink with the effort of keeping herself under control, but the chief was more prepared for her than any of us could imagine.

'Hands to the front,' he barked. 'Get them out.'

Viv held out her hands obediently, palms uppermost.

'Turn them over, Miss Tintoft,' the chief said impatiently, slapping his boot with his stick to indicate he was in no mood to be trifled with. 'You know perfectly well what I want to see.'

Viv turned over her hands. I saw with relief that the talons were no longer purple.

'Ah,' said the chief with satisfaction, 'I see that the varnish has been removed; all that remains now is for the nails to be trimmed.' To everyone's astonishment he put a hand into the pocket of his impeccably-cut tweed jacket and produced a pair of scissors. 'Will you do it or shall I?' he enquired.

Viv stared at him, aghast. She couldn't have looked any

more horrified if he had suggested amputation of the fingers. 'I'm not having them *cut*!' she yelped. 'It took me *years* to grow these!'

'Nevertheless, Miss Tintoft,' the chief said in a deadly voice, 'either you cut them or I shall. Alternatively, you may prefer to leave the training centre; but I assure you that you will not mount a horse in this establishment with fingernails resembling those of a Chinese mandarin.'

There was a tense silence as they faced each other, but at the end of it Viv sighed deeply and took the scissors. One by one the talons fell and vanished into the tan. The chief pocketed the scissors with a thin smile of satisfaction.

'Ride! TO HORSE!' he bellowed.

5

A Little Miracle

'Check your girths!'
  'Take your reins!'
  'Down irons!'
  'Prepare to mount!'
  'Ride – MOUNT!'
With the chief's instructions ringing in our ears like machine gun fire, we progressed into our saddles in a succession of jerks, like badly manipulated puppets. It was two years since I had received any formal instruction and I had been rather dreading this; afraid I would have forgotten all that I had learned.

'Leading file, prepare to lead off on the right rein!' bellowed the chief.

We all looked round anxiously and I saw with relief that I wasn't the only one to hesitate. Typically, Annemarie was the first to move forward, electing herself to the position of leading file.

'Ride – pre-pare to walk!'
  'Ride – WALK!'
Somehow we managed to achieve an orderly procession and the chief began to work us gently at the walk and trot through turns, circles and transitions, making no comment, but taking in every ill-timed movement of our hands and legs, every falter in our horses' strides with his gimlet eye.

In between concentrating on my own performance and trying to keep Legend on the track – he would have much preferred to give the kicking boards, with their painted letters, a wider berth, and I realized that he had probably never been ridden indoors in his life before – I studied the other scholarship students to see what sort of competition I was up against for a place in the team for the junior trial.

Annemarie, as one would expect from someone who had studied at the Reitschule, was a highly disciplined and faultlessly correct rider who clearly expected and extracted the same exact discipline from her little bay horse. If there was a criticism to be made it was that she seemed rather too stiff, a little too unyielding, and I noticed that for much of the time the bay gelding was slightly overbent with his chin tucked into his neck. I knew, even without seeing them perform, that they would be formidable competition for the dressage and the show-jumping, both of which demanded precision and total accuracy, but I was not so sure how they would fare across country when scope, speed, and initiative all had a part to play.

Alice had gained her early riding experience in a dealer's yard, and you could tell by the way she rode her huge, handsome, iron grey, The Talisman, that she was fearless. She had told us appalling stories of how she used to display the prowess of the equine merchandise by jumping them over some spiked iron railings into a municipal park. This had rarely failed to impress potential buyers and if any horse injured itself, it was shunted round the back of the premises and sold off cheaply to the trade as damaged stock. Obviously this sort of training had developed a natural tact, an ability to get the best performance out of any horse, and I reckoned that Alice and The Talisman would be hot stuff across country, but I looked at Alice's long, loose, style of riding, and I wondered about the dressage.

Selina's plain, three-quarter bred gelding was totally redeemed by the beauty of his colour, a hot, bright, deep chestnut, with not a white hair to be seen. His name was Flame Thrower and he looked a wise, sensible, bold horse, who reminded me very much of a horse that Hans Gelderhol had been eventing at the time I was in his yard training for my Horsemaster's Certificate. The resemblance was so striking that I made a mental note to ask Selina how he was bred, to find out if they were related. Selina was a good rider, who had obviously been very well taught; on top of everything else she seemed to have going for her, I found this rather irksome.

Viv rode just in front of me on her own chestnut, a long-striding, powerful horse called Balthazar, who walked with a swinging stride and carried his tail gaily. Viv rode him in a relaxed and stylish manner and they were so well matched that they were a pleasure to watch. In fact all of the scholarship students rode well and were a pleasure to watch, apart from Mandy, but then Mandy and her pretty bay horse, Fox Me, were something else.

How Mandy had ever managed to qualify for the scholarship course, or even achieve sixth place at the two-day event, seemed a mystery, because to watch her floundering aimlessly round the school, cutting the corners, staring wild-eyed at the chief whenever he barked out a command, falling further and further behind the ride until she suddenly realized and legged Fox Me on so urgently that he arrived abruptly with his nose bumping into Legend's tail, it was clear that she was a total stranger to formal riding instruction.

All this became eventually too much for the chief to endure and he was obliged to halt the ride and enquire waspishly if this was a special performance, or if she always rode like an Irish tinker. Mandy stared at him in terror, not knowing whether it was meant to be a compliment or not. The chief then proceeded to give her a lecture on the co-ordination of hand, leg and seat in order to produce a balanced, working pace which would enable her to keep up with the ride.

I was sure that most of this was lost on Mandy and I mentally crossed her off the list of possibles for the junior trial, feeling sure that her sixth place at the two-day event could have been nothing but a fluke. It was heartening to count up and realize that as there were five of us left, I could count on being reserve at least provided the final student did not turn up. I was in need of this sort of comfort because Legend, irritated by the sudden jostling of Fox Me, and not enjoying his taste of indoor life in the least, was not on top form.

The enclosed arena had put a constraint on him and I could feel that his paces were not as fluent and free as they usually were. It was also difficult to keep his attention as the slightest noise, a stirrup iron scraping along the kicking boards, or a bird fluttering in the rafters above, made him tense. When someone ran up the steps and along the gallery, which extended for the entire length of the building, he bunched up and bounced like a rubber ball into the centre of the school, momentarily displacing the chief from his central position.

'Control, Miss Elliot, control,' he said in an irritated voice, 'this is an assessment period, not *El Rodeo*.'

I coaxed Legend back on to the track, feeling humiliated. I knew that I must be making a very poor impression, second only in awfulness to Mandy. It even struck me that were the Fanes present to compare our performance with that of the others, they would probably decide on the spot that I was not a fit person to ride the horse in which they so tenaciously claimed an interest.

Troubled with such thoughts, I fell into line with the others as the chief set up two jumps, one at either end of the school, in order to assess our show-jumping prowess. It was at this particular moment that one of the sliding doors opened, causing Legend yet more anxiety, and a tall, lean, young man entered the school, leading a startling roan horse with white stockings extending to above every knee, a broad blaze between its wall eyes, and its tail carried as high as a banner.

We all stared. If the chief had considered Mandy's riding like that of an Irish tinker, then surely he was now faced with one in the flesh. The new arrival wore a faded brown riding hat with the ventilator button missing, a checked shirt with the sleeves rolled above slim, brown elbows, a red neckerchief, and skin-tight jodhpurs worn with short, beige, elastic-sided suede boots.

The chief straightened up with the cup and pin he had been attaching to the jump stand still in his hands. He threw up his chin. 'Entry to the indoor school is expressly forbidden whilst there is a lesson in progress,' he snapped. 'There is a notice posted on the door – I suggest you consult it.'

'But I'm supposed to be taking part in this lesson,' the young man protested in an impeccable voice which signified an expensively privileged education. 'I'm on the scholarship course; my name's Phillip Hastings.'

49

The chief looked fit to explode. 'Then, Mr Hastings,' he said, 'you will also be aware that you were supposed to arrive prior to six o'clock yesterday evening!'

'I got the wrong day, I'm afraid.' Phillip Hastings had the grace to look somewhat shamefaced. 'I thought it was today the course started. I actually thought I was early.'

The chief closed his eyes for a moment and then heaved a deep sigh of resignation. 'Mr Hastings,' he said, 'be good enough to remove that object from around your throat and this afternoon, ten minutes prior to the cross-country assessment, kindly present yourself for my inspection at the office correctly attired for formal instruction, wearing a collar and tie, a jacket, and *long* riding boots.'

The rest of us watched with interest whilst the chief made a rapid assessment of Phillip and the amazing roan horse as he drilled them round the partly constructed show-jumps. It was galling to see at once that there was another scholar-ship candidate who was sickeningly good, and that the roan horse, despite its eccentric and somewhat off-putting appearance, was fluent, obedient, and expertly schooled.

'He's one for the team, anyway,' Viv whispered, 'I'd lay a bet on it.' Forcing myself to agree with her in a matter-of-fact voice, I felt my heart sink like a lead weight in my chest.

Lunch, with Alice in charge of the catering, was not a success. Alice's idea of cookery was a fried egg slapped on to a piece of hard, blackened toast, and even this was not achieved without a lot of bad-tempered banging about and a haze of smoke, which hung above our heads as we waited uneasily at the table.

Selina, who had somehow managed to finish the assessment period looking as cool as a cucumber with not even the slightest of marks on her beautiful breeches, looked aggrieved as Alice thumped down the plates in front of us.

'Are *all* of the eggs broken?' she enquired.

They were, because Alice had not been able to find a spatula and had lifted them out of the pan with a dessert spoon. She had even managed to drop one of them on to the kitchen floor, but I only discovered this later when I happened to slip on the patch of grease it left behind.

Phillip, who didn't seem to object to the squalid interior and hideous surroundings of the Duke of Newcastle in the least, ate his egg without complaint. He told us that his father, who was insisting that Phillip went to university to study Law, had refused to finance his eventing on the grounds that it would interfere with his studies, but had been foiled by Phillip gaining a place on the scholarship course. If he could get a place in the team for the junior trial and be short-listed for the Junior Olympics, he hoped to use it as a lever to persuade his father that he was good enough to make a career out of eventing. 'But if I don't do it this time,' he told us, 'I'm sunk, because I'm due to take up my place at Magdalene in September.'

I couldn't help wondering what the Fellows of Magdalene would think of Phillip, because when he had removed his shabby riding hat, we discovered that he had dyed his forelock platinum blonde.

Viv, who had described to us how she had pasted her own hair with powdered bleach and hydrogen peroxide, and had sat for hours with her head wrapped in aluminium foil like a Christmas turkey before applying a henna rinse to achieve the present flaming orange colour, was quite jealous.

'What did you use?' she wanted to know. 'How long did it take?'

'Heavens, I didn't do it *myself*,' Phillip said, shocked by the thought. 'I had it done professionally at André Bernard.'

Annemarie succumbed to a choking fit at this piece of information and had to retire to the kitchen for a draught of cold water.

To finish the meal, Alice presented us with mugs of strong, thick coffee.

'What's this,' Selina wanted to know, 'gravy?'

'If you don't like it,' Alice said truculently, 'make your own.'

'I shall do that,' Selina said and, rising from her chair, she disappeared in the direction of the kitchen and returned shortly afterwards bearing recognizable coffee in a china cup and saucer. 'I took the precaution of bringing my own,' she explained. We couldn't help but be impressed. You had to hand it to Selina, she had thought of everything.

We rode out to the cross-country course after lunch, tweaking up our girths and checking that each other's bridle straps were tucked into their keepers. Phillip was now formally attired after being inspected and approved by the chief; I was wearing a shirt and tie; Selina had encased Mandy's floppy hair in one of her own nets; Annemarie was without her gold studs; and even Alice had cobbled a button on to her jacket and altered her boot straps, although whether or not she would see the nurse about her spots was open to conjecture.

We worked our horses in on the long sweep of grass that led into the first fence of the cross-country course. It was heaven to be riding outdoors again, and Legend obviously thought so as well because he seemed to be quite his usual eager self, flipping out his toes at the trot and bouncing off into canter, shaking his glossy bay neck and making his mane fly. Slowly, my confidence began to return.

The chief, who was concerned not to overtax our horses, most of whom had hardly settled in after their long journey the previous afternoon, gave us five fairly straightforward fences to jump for our assessment, comprising the first two and the final three obstacles of the full cross-country course. They consisted of a plain post and rail; a tiger trap – a triangle of dry pine poles which made a hollow noise when you tapped it; a sheep pen of wattle fencing; a bank of tractor tyres – wide ones on the bottom, narrowing to smaller car-sized tyres on the top, and ridged with a telegraph pole; and finally, a modest square-trimmed hedge. None of the fences was over three feet in height, although the tiger trap and the tyre fence had bases which stretched to five feet as we discovered when we were allowed, two at a time, with the others minding our horses, to walk the course.

Annemarie went first, achieving a clear and correct, if rather tight-fisted round, and Phillip followed, his roan displaying, as we had known it would, an effortless ability to clear the fences in a relaxed manner, which I saw by my stopwatch was also deceptively fast. I felt sure that Magdalene College had lost a law student, as Phillip seemed a certainty for the junior trial and even the Olympic short-list.

Selina went next on Flame Thrower and theirs was a cool, professional performance, lacking only the drive and urgency of the real thing. Viv and Balthazar started off at a powerful canter which increased in speed as they went, too fast, into the sheep pen and Balthazar took the second wattle fence with his back legs, detaching it from its roped moorings. This meant a delay for Alice and The Talisman, who had been circling round the starting point. Viv cantered back to us with a rueful grin and a nonchalant lift of her shoulders.

'She'll never make the team with that attitude,' Annemarie commented, 'she didn't even bother to judge her strides. She just left it to the horse; she couldn't care less. She wouldn't have lasted five minutes at the Reitschule.'

'Oh, *wouldn't* I?' Viv interspersed from behind somewhat unexpectedly, as Alice and The Talisman thundered past us on their way to the first fence. 'Well, we shall see, won't we, when the team is announced, whether the Reitschule has done *you* any good or not!'

As it was my turn next, I removed myself hastily from what promised to develop into a lively argument, and took Legend away to warm up. As we circled round, I saw The Talisman flatten the second half of the sheep pen and caught a glimpse of the chief's agonized expression as he went forward to strap it yet again. I could see that combination fences were going to be troublesome for The Talisman and Balthazar, both bold, strong, free-striding horses with a common disregard for anything less substantial than a telegraph pole.

When the chief raised his arm as a signal for me to start, I cantered Legend strongly towards the post and rails, he jumped it easily and leapt onwards, his eyes already fixed on the tiger trap. He extended into it and flew over and we turned towards the sheep pen. I steadied him, sitting down hard in the saddle, determined not to go into it too fast, because Legend, although not as big as either Balthazar or The Talisman, could produce a huge raking stride where necessary, and I had already paced out the pen and decided that two shorter strides would be preferable to negotiate the second half with absolute accuracy. So I held him back, releasing him for the first half, but not so much that I couldn't get the two canter strides inside to meet the wattle fence perfectly. We sailed out and on over the tractor tyres and the clipped hedge in triumph, and as we cantered back to the others, I slapped Legend's neck gratefully, feeling him vindicated from the morning's disastrous performance.

'Come back, Miss Elliot,' shouted the chief, 'and give me one stride at the sheep pen!'

I turned Legend back and my feeling of exhilaration died as we approached the pen again, knowing that of all the students who had gone so far, none had been asked to take the fence again. I pushed Legend on hard and he responded magnificently, thrusting forward with his powerful hocks, his front legs flying. He soared up and over the first wattle, took one flying stride in between and rose over the second like a bird. Well, I thought, as we trotted round the tractor tyres without a backward glance, if the chief had wanted one stride, we had certainly given him one. He didn't call us back a second time.

Mandy was last. We all stood with our hearts in our mouths as she cantered Fox Me towards the first fence, expecting her to fall off or let the horse refuse. He sailed over. He did the same at the tiger trap, and they turned towards the wattle sheep pen and jumped it neatly and effortlessly as if it had been no more than a couple of cavelletti. We were stunned.

The chief was clearly stunned as well because, when the pair finished, he called them back to do it again. Fox Me faced the post and rails for a second time without the least hesitation, he sailed into the tiger trap with total confidence and no thought of refusal, while Mandy, with absolute faith in his ability, and hindering him not one whit by superfluous aid or instruction, sat aboard him, radiant.

The chief was visibly perplexed by the problem this

presented to him as an instructor in the fine art of equitation. One could see that whilst on the one hand his impeccable standards of excellence were appalled by Mandy's passive and untutored method of riding, his instinct made him reluctant to interfere with the fragile balance of their totally successful partnership, lest he destroy with discipline and conventional technique something which was god-given and somehow sobering to watch.

Much as the chief must have itched to tear Mandy's riding apart, and make her begin again from the basics, he resisted it totally. For the whole of the course he made only minor adjustments to her riding position, for the sake of her chances of gaining a place in the team, and out of respect for a partnership based on a perfect understanding.

Seeing all this take place served to increase my respect for the chief albeit, after the incident at the double, somewhat reluctantly. It was inspiring to realize that even he could recognize a little miracle when he saw one. But watching Mandy and Fox Me negotiate the sheep pen smoothly for the second time, and pondering upon the slightly unwelcome possibility that they were now back on my list of possibles for selection, I felt in need of a little miracle myself.

6

Once More, With Feeling . . .

By the end of the first week, we had settled into our daily routine. We stumbled out of bed to the shrilling of many alarms at a quarter to six, gulped a cup of coffee, and clad in the stable workers' uniform of jeans, long rubber boots, and lovat anoraks or quilted waistcoats, set off for the yards alongside the working pupils and the early duty staff. Our first job was to muck out our horses and scrub out and refill the water buckets. Then we removed the horses' night rugs, gave them a brief grooming, which included washing off any dirty patches, picking out their feet, brushing straw out of their tails, and laying their manes, and we put on their day rugs. Whilst all this was going on, a numbered and weighed hay net was delivered, and a muck cart, pulled by a mini-tractor, collected the dirty bedding stacked neatly on a spread sack outside each stable.

Feeding followed; the feeds mixed in accordance with the charts devised by the chief detailing individual menus for each horse. While the horses ate their breakfast we helped to rake and sweep the yards, until not an alien speck or wisp remained for the chief to see when he carried out his daily inspection.

At eight thirty we scholarship students were scheduled for our half-hour run around the perimeter of the cross-country course. This was supervised by a member of staff to make sure we didn't cheat. For the first few days this was simply murder; we staggered along with aching calves, gasping breath and stitches, limping back to the Duke of Newcastle in agony. Naturally, only Selina had managed to come properly equipped with running shoes. The rest of us had to make do with rubber boots, jodhpur boots, or shoes that managed to be even less suitable. Nevertheless by the end of the week most of us were beginning to find it less of a strain and more enjoyable – all except for Mandy, who flopped along behind looking absolutely exhausted.

After the run we had breakfast – the box marked PROVISIONS FOR THE DUKE OF NEWCASTLE never failed to appear on the doorstep whilst early morning stables was in progress. By nine thirty we were back on the yards. A thorough strapping for the horses was the first task, from whence we were called away individually to endure ten minutes lunging on a round, piebald, pony who appeared to do little else but trot and canter round in circles every day of his life. We swung our arms and legs and did various exercises designed to supple us, improve our balance, and strengthen and deepen our seats. All it did for us at first was to increase our aches and stiffness. The lunging period, according to the chief's daily schedule, was to be extended by ten minutes every week until in the last week we were being lunged for forty minutes each day. The thought of it, as we reeled away after just ten minutes, was frightening.

At eleven o'clock we had to be tacked up for our first lesson of the day which was usually dressage, followed by a circuit of the show-jumping arena, and at twelve thirty we rugged up our horses again, skipped out their boxes, fed them, and went for lunch.

We were out on the yards again at two to prepare for the afternoon's cross-country instruction, during which the chief cruised between fences in a Range Rover. It was a two-hour period, but as a lot of it comprised standing about and discussing technique, it was not too taxing, and at four thirty we returned to the yards, and were allowed half an hour's break for tea. At five we skipped out the stables again, shook out the horses' beds for the night, topped up their water buckets, changed day rugs for jute rugs, the evening feeds were mixed and another hay net delivered, and the yards were raked and swept again for the chief's evening inspection at six.

After supper we reported to the tack room to clean our saddlery in order that the whole procedure should be repeated again the following day, and although there was still lots of activity going on in the yard – horse boxes and trailers constantly coming and going as outsiders brought along their own horses for evening instruction, and we were allowed to watch the lessons from the gallery, or from a vantage point on the cross-country course if we wished – all we ever wanted to do in the first week was to plod wearily back to the Duke of Newcastle and fall into bed.

On Saturday morning I had a letter from Nick. It read:

Dear Elaine,

Thanks for sending the garage – I really enjoyed my three-hour wait. Lots of cars came along between the time you abandoned me and the arrival of the truck, but I didn't flag them down because I knew you'd remember me eventually – if I waited long enough (story of my life).

Typically, the Fanes were unsympathetic when I got back, implying that the puncture must have been our fault – well, you know the Fanes . . . but you'll be pleased to hear I didn't lose my temper. I did tackle them about your wages, but only time will tell if it did any good.

I'll call in and have another go at them because I understand the new girl has moved in, and I want to see is she's the wonder woman she's made out to be (might also be pretty), and I'll tell you the news when I see you, which will be on Monday – I'll call for you at 2.30 P.M., and don't say you can't because I know you've got an afternoon off, I checked.

Trusting you're top of the class,

Love etc,

Nick.

I had very mixed feelings about this. Nick had dropped off the remainder of my things late on Sunday evening after the garage had fixed the horsebox. At the time, he had still obviously felt very piqued about the incident because he had simply left the box of equipment in the yard, from where I had retrieved it the following morning. I had been feeling guilty about not remembering to call the garage earlier and had been meaning to ring and apologize. Somehow, there had not been the time and I was pleased that he had written now and relieved that he had apparently forgiven me.

His reference to the Fanes, though, stirred up unwelcome emotions. I had been too busy to give them much thought in the past week. While I certainly did not want to hear about the new wonder woman, because I felt that the wages the Fanes were paying her were rightfully mine, I was dismayed to discover that I felt jealous at the thought of someone else grooming and exercising the horses that I had loved – and I *had* loved them, even though I was only now beginning to realize just how much.

After lunch on Saturday, we discussed the technique of jumping fences involving water, and now we stood in a group and watched Selina and Flame Thrower approaching a telegraph pole situated in the middle of a small lake which necessitated jumping into and out of two feet of water. For once, Selina was in trouble. She had entered the lake too slowly and too cautiously, and Flame Thrower, having allowed himself to be ridden into the lake, noticed the telegraph pole too late to be reconciled to it. He refused.

The chief, standing on the bank with his beautiful boots inches from the water and with a tweed cap on his head, hailed her irritably: 'Back, Miss Gibbons, come back! Try again from the rise; this time with more impulsion!'

Selina turned the bright chestnut horse away from the pole and they splashed towards the bank. Flame Thrower's tail hung in a sodden lump, and Selina's beautiful breeches were becoming wetter by the minute. They set off again from the rise, cantering into the water and throwing up clouds of spray, but the chief was having none of it.

'Impulsion, Miss Gibbons,' he bellowed, 'does *not* mean you merely increase the speed!'

Selina halted the horse's progress towards the obstacle and they foundered through the water towards the chief. By this time they were both dripping wet.

'I am perfectly aware of that,' Selina said in an incensed voice, 'perfectly. But it is extremely difficult to work up either enthusiasm *or* impulsion, when one is drenched with filthy water, and the horse does not like the look of the obstacle one is approaching one little bit.'

Surprisingly, the chief didn't lose his temper; in fact, he seemed to find Selina's obvious discomfort rather amusing. 'Quite,' he said, 'but if you expect to be accepted as a serious candidate for the junior trial, you must imagine that you are riding for your country; you must ride as if your life depended upon it; you must ride at that obstacle with body and soul united in determination to get over – even if you are killed in the attempt.'

Selina stared at him with pursed lips. 'I came on this course for the good of my career,' she said. 'I didn't realize I would be expected to die for my country.' Nevertheless, she turned Flame Thrower away and set off again from the rise. This time she gave it everything she had and they sailed over. The chief sent her back to the yard to change her clothes.

The next fence presented a different problem, being an uphill double. The chief began with a lecture on gradients, explaining how the horse's stride naturally lengthened going downhill and shortened going up. He made us dismount and pace the distance between the rails on foot. Each rider, he said, should be familiar with the natural length of their horse's stride, and, by taking into consideration the gradient and the speed, should calculate whether it would be sensible to achieve four long, six short, or whatever other combination of strides were necessary in order to present the horse correctly at the second part of the double.

Viv went first on Balthazar. They approached it at a powerful gallop which shook the ground, flew over the first part, took three huge, raking strides, and finding themselves still inconveniently far away from the second part, chanced it anyway with a vast leap which, though mighty and courageous in its attempt, could not be high enough to clear the top rail. Balthazar hit the timber with an impact that would have knocked the hind legs off a lesser animal, and cantered back to us with not so much as a mark on his cannon bones.

The chief was furious, and told us that if the fence had come towards the end of the course, and taking into consideration horse and rider fatigue and the gradient involved, to attempt to take a solidly fixed double at such a punishing pace would be a recipe for disaster; the result of which would probably be two broken legs for the horse and a broken neck for the rider. After a short interval spent trotting in circles to ascertain that Balthazar was indeed still sound, he dispatched them to try again, and this time they approached it at a more sober pace, achieving four comfortable strides between the fences and two clean jumps.

Alice went next on The Talisman, who was very enthusiastic about his jumping and not easily controlled. He got away from Alice on the approach, threw up his head and raced at the double, landing a long way in. This upset Alice's stride calculations, and as she struggled to check him, he hesitated, put in an extra one, and took off too close to the second part, slamming the rails with both pairs of fetlocks and almost pitching Alice over his head as he landed. He trotted back to us on three legs with blood welling from his off-hind coronet.

Alice flung herself out of the saddle and knelt to examine the damage. 'I knew damned well he wasn't going to make it as soon as we took off,' she said in an angry voice. The chief sighed and ordered her back to the yard to seek medication.

Phillip and the amazing roan went through the double in perfect copy-book style and they were followed by Annemarie and her little bay horse. It was clear that he would have attempted to jump over the moon if she had asked him, but the fact that he was small and close-coupled, meant she had to jump him with deadly accuracy and place him every inch of the way. This suited her disciplined way of riding but it meant that they were slow, and I had noticed that the little horse had been at full stretch when we were working over spreads. Brave as a lion he might be, but even his courage and Annemarie's ambitious determination couldn't give him the scope he lacked to turn him into the potential top class event horse she so desperately wanted him to be. He would do his best, but it was clear, as we watched him, that as the fences got higher and wider, and as the pace got faster, his best wouldn't be good enough. The only person who didn't see this, or who wouldn't allow herself to see it, was Annemarie.

Mandy followed Annemarie, and although she appeared to close her eyes and leave it all to Fox Me, he leapt the first part, and with four swinging, perfectly judged strides, met the second part exactly right and soared over. There was nothing the chief could say to this so he said nothing.

It was my turn last of all. I had worked out that Legend, who had a naturally long, floating stride, would shorten due to the gradient, taking four normal uphill strides inside the double, bringing himself exactly right for the second half without any adjustment from me. Being an economist by nature, I could see no justification in asking for shortened and lengthened strides if the same result could be accomplished more effortlessly without. It seemed that my calculations were right, because Legend did it beautifully and as he swept through the double it felt deceptively easy. It probably looked too easy as well because the chief sent us to do it again, this time with instructions to get three long strides between the fences.

I felt this was a bit unreasonable, especially as he had been furious with Viv for attempting it, but I knew Legend could do it and I took him at it from a good distance away, feeling the power from his hocks and the thrust of his shoulders as he flew forward. He rose over the first part, and with my legs clasped urgently to his sides, he flew onwards with three enormous strides that ate up the ground, soared over the second part and landed perfectly. It was simply marvellous.

'Now do it again,' the chief commanded, 'and give me five short bounces.'

I couldn't believe it. I trotted Legend up to him feeling indignant. 'But I've already been over it *twice*,' I said, 'and he's done it beautifully both times.'

'Allow me to be the judge of that, Miss Elliot,' the chief snapped. 'This time I want to see you take it slowly, with lots of impulsion, and absolute control.'

I could hardly refuse. I rode back to the approach line, gritting my teeth, bursting to retort that I had been in absolute control both of the previous times.

I sent Legend forward towards the double yet again, but this time, because he would have liked to race at it as before, I sat down hard and held him back, feeling the stretched muscles and tendons pulling in my calves and my heels, and the energy being contained by the reins until it was as if I held a coiled spring in my hands. Legend's dark hooves pounded on the turf, his neck arched and his ears strained forward. I placed him at the first part, releasing him only enough to allow him to jump, collected him, held him for one, two, three, four, five, short, bouncing strides, released him dangerously near to the second part, and up he went, up almost like a lift, and over, tucking up his hind legs to clear the rail. We had done it. I looked at the chief in triumph, but he was already waving me on towards the next fence. 'Ride on! Ride on!' he shouted. 'Continue over the next jump.' He didn't even say well done.

I rode on feeling angry. I didn't know why the chief should be trying to humiliate me, but I felt he had sent us again and again at the double in the hope that eventually we would make a mistake. Well, we hadn't. I was fiercely proud of Legend and I leaned forward in the saddle and rubbed his neck with my knuckles as we cantered on up the rise. 'We'll show the chief,' I told him, 'we'll get fitter than the others, we'll work harder than the others, and we'll make the team, he'll *have* to choose us. Then we'll show *everybody* what we can do.'

We thudded towards the brush fence situated on top of the rise, and suddenly Legend began to falter in his stride. This was very out of character as he wasn't the sort of horse to spook at a perfectly straightforward fence, but he would certainly have stopped had I not legged him on energetically. He took off with reluctance and might even have turned back in mid-air had it been at all possible, due to the surprising nature of what lay behind.

Two people were standing beside the wings. They were Nigella and Henrietta Fane.

7

Where Own Horse Welcomed

I managed to pull Legend up after a few strides and I stared at them, speechless.

'I don't know why you're looking at us like that,' Henrietta said in an annoyed tone, 'you knew we were coming; we said we would bring your wages.'

'They said in the office it would be perfectly all right to come up here,' Nigella said, 'as long as we kept out of sight, and didn't get in the way.' She wore a vast, shapeless jersey above some grubby lilac culottes, and below them, her hunting boots.

As I still hadn't said anything, Henrietta said, 'I suppose you do still *want* your wages? Nick seemed to think you were pretty desperate.'

'Why,' I asked her, 'have you brought them?' I looked at her suspiciously because I didn't actually believe it.

'Of course we've brought them,' Nigella said, 'why else would we be here?'

'Other than to see Legend, of course,' Henrietta put in swiftly, in case for one moment I might imagine they had softened in their attitude.

'Well, if you *have* brought my wages,' I said, 'I would rather like to have them, please.'

Henrietta pulled a crumpled brown envelope with a window in it out of her appallingly ancient anorak. She held it out to me wordlessly and I took it from her.

'We haven't managed to pay you everything that we owe you,' Nigella was forced to admit now that she was faced with the presence of the envelope, 'but we did manage to pay you half – well,' she added, as I took out and counted the five ten pound notes it contained, 'almost half.'

Inside the envelope there was also a folded piece of paper. I opened it out, expecting it to be an IOU, but it was no such thing, it was a garage bill.

<pre>
To recovery of Horse Box
registration number
SPD 347W   £24.50

To repairs to two
punctured tyres   4.20

V.A.T. at 15%   4.30
                                    £33.00
</pre>

'I think this belongs to you,' I said. I held it out to Henrietta.

She made no move to take it.

'Now look here,' I said angrily, 'you don't actually expect me to pay the garage bill out of my own wages? *I'm* not responsible for the upkeep of the horsebox. It wasn't *my* fault the spare tyre hadn't been repaired!'

There was at this point an approaching thunder of hooves, which necessitated a timely removal of ourselves to a safe distance in order to avoid being trampled by Phillip Hastings and his amazing roan horse.

We watched him rise up over the brush and canter strongly onwards before we resumed our conversation.

'But Elaine,' Nigella protested, 'if you hadn't used the box to come to the training centre, the second puncture might never have happened and the clients would have had the spare repaired. *We* wouldn't have been expected to pay.'

'But you expect *me* to pay,' I blazed back at them furiously. 'Even though you claim to have a financial interest in my horse, you don't seem at all keen to share responsibility when it actually comes to parting with hard cash!'

'We weren't supposed to have been using the horsebox at all,' Henrietta countered angrily. 'We only allowed you to use it out of kindness. If you had hired a box it would have cost twice that much!'

'And as you hadn't paid me any wages for six months,' I said bitterly, 'you knew I couldn't do that.'

There was a dreadful silence after this broken by the sound of more hooves as Viv and Balthazar breasted the fence and pounded onwards.

'What have you come for, anyway?' I asked them in a dispirited voice.

'We came to bring your wages,' Nigella said, 'we came to see how you were, to see Legend, and to tell you our new girl has started and that things are looking up for us.'

'She's shutting off half of the park so that we can make our own hay for the winter,' Henrietta said in a satisfied tone. 'She's giving riding lessons on the hirelings, *and* we're to take horses for breaking and schooling. That's not to mention the grass liveries; we've already got two of those.'

'In other words,' I said, annoyed, 'you've come to gloat.'

'Not gloat, Elaine,' Nigella protested, 'we just thought you'd like to know how things are, so you won't feel so guilty about leaving us in the lurch.'

'Nigella,' I said crossly, 'I don't *feel* guilty about leaving you in the lurch.'

'Oh yes you do,' Henrietta said, 'Nick told us.'

I stared at her angrily, wounded to think that Nick had seen fit to repeat what I had regarded as our private conversation.

Annemarie came over the brush, glaring at us as she cantered past. The little bay's neck was ridged with wrinkles due to being held so furiously in check. Legend began to sidle and shake his head, anxious to be away.

'As you will shortly be very prosperous due to all this increased business,' I said, 'perhaps you'll feel able to drop your ridiculous claim to a share in my horse, especially as you've replaced me so advantageously that you'll never need my services again.'

Henrietta frowned. 'Why should we,' she demanded, 'when we're entitled to it?'

'It isn't just the money, Elaine,' Nigella pointed out, 'we don't want to jeopardize your career in the least. We *like* having an interest in an event horse, it's opened up a whole new world for us. We've never had more fun than we've had in the last eighteen months.'

Henrietta made no move to agree. She stared down at her sawn-off wellingtons, the toes mended by means of a patch from a cycle puncture repair kit. If this was true, she wasn't going to allow me the satisfaction of hearing her say it.

'And we're all so looking forward to coming to the junior trial,' Nigella continued, adding anxiously, 'you will want us to come, won't you . . . it will be all right, won't it?' As I made no reply but continued to stare angrily at Henrietta, she blurted out, 'Mummy told me to say she misses you *terribly*.'

I didn't want to hear this. I didn't want to hear any of it; not how much Lady Jennifer was missing me, not how the new girl was going to achieve miracles – miracles that if I had stayed and been less determined to pursue my own eventing career, I might have achieved myself. 'I have to go now,' I said, 'I'm supposed to be under instruction and already the chief will be wondering where I am.' I made to turn Legend away.

Henrietta looked up. She eyed me in a speculative manner. 'I suppose you've already got a new job organized for when you finish the course?' she said. 'We haven't actually seen your advertisement in *Horse & Hound*, but we could have missed it, of course.'

'I suppose you *have* advertised, Elaine?' Nigella said in a worried voice. 'Because with only three weeks to go, there isn't a lot of time left.'

I didn't need Nigella to tell me this and I didn't want the Fanes to know I hadn't placed an advertisement yet. Nor did I want to admit, even to myself, that the reason I had hesitated was that I had hoped that their new groom would be useless, and that they would beg me to go back. Despite the awfulness of Havers Hall, despite the way they had behaved over Legend and my wages, I realized that I was missing *them* terribly – Lady Jennifer, the horses – *my* horses – and even the Fanes themselves. But nothing, nothing in the world, would have allowed me to confess it, and so I lied. 'Yes,' I said, 'I advertised under a box number. I've found a place.'

There was a silence. Then: 'I expect they offered you better wages than ours,' Henrietta said in a quizzing tone.

'Since I wasn't shown your advertisement, I wouldn't know

what wages you offered,' I snapped, 'but I'm sure it wouldn't be difficult to offer better wages than you paid *me*.'

'Well, if you're going to be like that about it,' Henrietta retorted, 'if you don't want us to know what you *do* consider to be a decent wage, I'm sure we don't want to know anyway. I'm sure we're not all that interested.'

'As a matter of fact,' I told her, 'I'm getting fifty pounds a week.'

'Fifty pounds a week!' Nigella gasped. 'Really?'

'And free board and lodging and keep for Legend,' I added.

'Goodness,' Nigella exclaimed, 'we can't really compete with anything like that.'

'And time off for eventing?' Henrietta enquired.

'And time off for eventing,' I said.

'And use of a horsebox?'

'And use of a horsebox.'

'With a room of your own, not having to share with others?'

'Yes.'

'Heavens,' said Henrietta. I could see she was having difficulty in swallowing all this, which was hardly surprising since it sounded unlikely, even to my own ears.

'Where is it?' she said.

'Where is what?' I said, holding up Legend who was by now digging a hole in the turf with an impatiently flailing foreleg.

'The job, where *is* the job? Which county?'

'Oh,' I said vaguely, 'I've got a choice of two or three similar places and I haven't decided which to take yet.'

Nigella suddenly turned away. 'When you go,' she said in a strained little voice, 'you will leave us a forwarding address, won't you? We don't want to lose touch.'

'Because of Legend,' Henrietta added quickly, before I could think it was me they wanted to keep in touch with. 'We shall need to know where he is.'

For some appallingly sentimental reason my eyes suddenly filled with tears and I jerked Legend away almost roughly. I said, 'I really do have to go now. I'll see you at the trial, I expect.'

Mandy and Fox Me now appeared over the brush and I loosed Legend to canter after them.

'Elaine . . .' Nigella began in a choked voice as we bounded past, 'we . . .' but I couldn't turn back and, blinking hard, I rode on in a wide arc, past the brush fence to be confronted with the Range Rover bumping along gently, followed by the rest of the class.

'Fall in, Miss Elliot,' the chief barked from the driver's window. 'I want to see you take the brush again, and this time I want to see a more decisive approach; I want to see *positive, controlled* horsemanship.'

I trotted Legend back down the rise and set his head towards the brush once more. This time he didn't hesitate, and when we landed, the Fanes were nowhere to be seen.

Later the same day, when I returned to the Duke of Newcastle after the evening stint of tack cleaning, I found a piece of the Fanes' ancient notepaper with a crest on it in the bottom of my suitcase, borrowed Viv's ballpoint pen, and I was just about to help myself to an envelope from the stack of papers beneath Selina's bed, where she also kept her typewriter and a professional-looking camera, when the bedroom door opened.

'Elaine!' Selina exclaimed in a shocked voice. 'How *could* you snoop into my private belongings, when I have *expressly* asked you not to!'

I got up, feeling guilty. 'I'm not snooping,' I said defensively, 'I'm only desperate for an envelope. I've got a very important letter to write and when I tried to ask for one, you were on the pay phone in the lecture hall and you waved me away.'

Observing that I hadn't disturbed her stack of type-written papers, Selina softened. 'Well, you may have an envelope, of course,' she said sweetly, 'but please remember never to touch my belongings again. I do set a very high value on personal privacy.'

From the way she locked me out of our bedroom when she

was busily engaged on her typewriter I knew this to be true, so I took the proffered envelope with suitably humble thanks and left her to it.

I went into the sitting room and sat at the formica-topped table. Alice sat at the other end reading a romantic novel with a lurid cover, absently picking at her spots. Mandy sat in front of the electric fire, its one bar glowing bravely, with her Sony Walkman clamped over her floppy hair. Annemarie was slumped in an armchair, deep into *Die Klassiche Reitkunst*. Phillip and Viv were in the kitchen making toast and coffee.

Painstakingly I began to word my advertisement:

Experienced girl groom, Horsemaster's Cert., prepared to consider any situation where own horse welcomed. Write Box . . .

8
Washday

'Do you have to get a job to go to after the course?' Viv wanted to know as, after morning stables on Monday, we prepared for our stint at the washing rota. 'What about your old man? Couldn't you go back to him for a bit?' She raised her head from the collection of empty Vim cannisters, rusting Brillopads and dried up tins of boot polish which cluttered the clammy little cupboard under the kitchen sink. She handed me a packet of detergent.

I thought of my father and his little terraced town house with its minute paved backyard, 'my patio,' he called it, his rented garage three streets away which housed his beloved Morris Minor, twenty years old and still, as he proudly boasted, 'in showroom condition,' and his modest building society savings account. We lived in different worlds my father and I, and I knew I could never go back.

'There's nowhere to keep Legend,' I said, 'my father doesn't really like horses, and I know he'll think I'm crazy when I tell him I'm not going back to the Fanes. He thinks they're wonderful, especially Lady Jennifer.' The detergent was set into a solid brick. I tore off its cardboard wrapping, laid it on the draining board and began to break it up with a fork. 'No, I'll have to get a job, it's the only answer.'

Viv slammed the cupboard doors shut and straightened up. She trundled the old-fashioned twin-tub washing machine out of its corner, causing alarm amongst a family of spiders. 'Perhaps we should swop fathers for a while, you and me,' she suggested. 'My old man may have the money, but yours sounds as if he's got the sense to leave you to live your own life.' She connected the hose to the tap and turned on the water.

I looked at her, interested. 'You mean if you hadn't got the scholarship, you could still have had the training anyway?' I hadn't realized that there was so much money to

71

be made out of selling Indian sandles and belts, and I thought it fortunate that Alice didn't know of it because she was always making snide remarkes in front of Selina about people who could afford to pay taking up places on scholarships designed for those who couldn't.

'I could, but it's got to the stage where I won't take his money, so I probably wouldn't have.'

'But you do *want* to event?'

She shrugged her narrow shoulders in a typical gesture as we watched the water splash into the machine. 'How does anyone know *what* they want,' she said, 'especially with an old man like mine, always interfering, making arrangements, paying for things; finishing school, a hairdressing course, a secretarial course. I've hopped out of them all, but he never gives up, and now I've got Balthazar. It started off with just a few riding lessons, then a better instructor, then suddenly I'd got this horse, the best horse money could buy, and it seemed a waste really, not to event, because everyone said he could do it, and here I am . . .' she looked at me in genuine despair. 'If only he'd just leave me alone and give me a chance to decide what *I* want to do.'

I sprinkled some lumpy detergent into the water and it whirled round on the top, partly submerged, like a cluster of icebergs. 'But surely,' I said, 'you wouldn't put up with all this,' I waved an arm around the Duke of Newcastle's incredibly squalid little kitchen, 'and the work, and the running, and the lunging, and everything, if you didn't *want* to do it? No one would.'

As the water began to steam, she looked up and gave me an elfin grin. 'Ah, well, that's my competitive spirit asserting itself, isn't it? I'm going to get into the team now, just to spite Annemarie and the bloody Reitschule. Just for the satisfaction of seeing her face when the chief reads out my name and not hers; because that little Hanoverian of hers isn't going to make it, he hasn't got the scope.'

We began to load the first wash into the machine, and I reflected that already intense rivalries had sprung up between the scholarship students, between Alice and Selina, and between Viv and Annemarie who had only shared a cell for one night before war had been declared. Now Annemarie shared with Mandy, and Viv with Alice.

'Anyway,' Viv declared, 'I'm glad you haven't got too much money, Elaine, because money spoils. It changes your values, and, if you haven't actually earned it yourself, it stunts your growth and makes you lose your direction until, in the end, you doubt your own ability and lose your self respect.' She grabbed a pair of jeans out of my hands before they hit the water. 'Don't put *those* in – they'll dye everything blue!'

I could see that this might well be true, but it didn't stop me wishing I had some money; just enough to pay off the Fanes and to secure a roof over our heads for me and for Legend. 'What about your mother?' I wondered. 'Do you get on all right with her?' My own mother had left home, for a man fifteen years her junior, when I was ten.

Water suddenly began to fly about and splash over the sides of the machine although the lumps of detergent still bobbed on the top in an unpromising manner. I slapped on the lid, hoping to contain it.

'My mother's dead,' Viv said gloomily. 'If she'd been alive things would be different – we got on famously, my mum and I. She didn't expect me to be anything other than what I was, what I wanted to be, but my old man married again and I've got a stepmother now – oh, you should see her Elaine, she really thinks she's somebody and I *hate* her. She hates me as well but she pretends she doesn't, so I won't live at home any more. I live with my gran. The old man hates it and he's forever trying to get her to send me back, but she won't, and I won't go back, not while *she's* there, I couldn't stand it.' She grinned at me, her humour suddenly restored. 'So there you have it, but don't tell anyone, Elaine,' she warned, 'I'll skin you if you do!'

'I wouldn't,' I protested, 'I promise I won't say a word.'

The washing machine now began to vibrate in an alarming way and to creep across the kitchen until it reached the limit of its cable where it rattled and fretted with impotent fury. We halted its progress by propping a corner with *Die Klassiche Reitkunst*.

After a noisy interval the machine turned itself off with a small bang. I lifted the lid cautiously. The clothes were bound together in a distressingly tangled lump, speckled with undissolved detergent.

'We can't have got it hot enough,' Viv concluded. She turned the dial on the side of the machine to BOIL. I watched with some trepidation as the water began to bubble and steam billowed, but at last the speckles turned to suds. 'That's done it,' Viv said in a satisfied voice. 'It'll be done in no time.'

Soapsuds worked their way between the lid and the top of the machine, inching slowly down the sides and threatening the safety of *Die Klassiche Reitkunst*, then, with a mighty whooshing of the rinse and more furious vibratings, they were banished and the cycle came to an abrupt end. We pulled out the jumble of clothes and put them into the spinner. They seemed terribly hot.

'They certainly look clean, anyhow,' Viv observed as she transferred them to the laundry basket, then abruptly her tone changed. 'Cor, strike a light, Elaine,' she groaned, 'just take a look at these.'

I looked over her shoulder and saw that she was holding up Selina's beautiful breeches. They were hardly recognizable. All the lovely soft creamy suede strappings had shrunk to a quarter of their original size; not only that, but they were transformed into something utterly repulsive, dark and slippery and slimy to the touch, like raw pig's liver.

'It must be because we boiled them,' I said, appalled, 'they're ruined!' It was small consolation to look at the rest of the breeches and see that they had survived because they had self-strappings.

'We'll have to do something,' Viv said, 'Selina will go mad. She'll go absolutely barmy.'

We couldn't think of anything. We stood in the steamed up kitchen and we stared at the breeches, aghast.

'We'll try drying them,' Viv declared. 'First we'll get them dry, then we'll iron them out flat, but we'll stretch them as much as we can now, whilst they're still wet.'

We pulled at the breeches until we heard the stitching

74

begin to pop, then we fetched the electric fire and held the strappings as close to it as we dared. With the steam from the machine and the hot clothes and the strappings, the Duke of Newcastle's kitchen turned into a turkish bath, the windows poured. My hair hung lank to my shoulders and Viv's orange spikes stood on end so that she resembled a frightened cockatoo. In spite of all this the strappings were no better when they were dry. In fact they were worse. They toasted to a crisp and when we tried to iron out the crinkles, they broke up like biscuits. It was simply terrible.

There was only one thing to do. I ran for my cell, rummaged through my drawer and found my own identical breeches lying in their tissue, lovingly wrapped against their day of glory, and I substituted them for Selina's ruined ones. Viv crept out of the Duke of Newcastle's back door and buried the remains of the old ones in the muckheaps with the fish slice.

'There's a *devastatingly* handsome young man asking for you in the yard, Elaine,' Selina beamed round the door of our cell as I brushed my hair and fixed it with a slide. 'Have you known him long?' She came in and settled herself on her bed in anticipation of some interesting gossip. For someone who could be incredibly tart with anyone she suspected of showing an interest in her affairs, she showed an extraordinary curiosity about every last detail of other people's lives, and never tired of asking questions.

'About eighteen months,' I said. 'He works for the Midvale and Westbury Hunt.'

'Does he really,' she said, impressed, 'and does he wear scarlet? I should think he would look simply divine in scarlet.'

'Yes, he wears scarlet,' I said, 'he's first whipper-in.'

'Oh, how marvellous!' Selina clasped her hands together and looked beatific. 'And is it unbearably romantic?'

I remembered the mud, and the lost shoes, and the rain, and Nelson's saddle, black, like old washleather. 'No,' I said, 'not very, it's a plough country.'

'Not the hunting,' Selina said crossly, 'I mean the relationship.'

'Oh,' I said in a shocked voice, 'I couldn't *possibly* tell you that. I set rather a high value on personal privacy.' I snatched up my good navy guernsey and smiled at her vexed expression as I made for the door.

I walked through the yards, looking for Nick. Everywhere was unusually quiet as Monday was a rest day at the training centre; no horses were exercised, no lessons were given, and only a skeleton staff were retained in order to feed, water, and attend to basic necessary duties. I looked in to see Legend on my way past his box, but he was busy with a hay net and couldn't be bothered with any acknowledgement other than the cock of an ear in my direction.

Nick was waiting in the car park, leaning with his elbows on the roof of his white sports car, and smoking a cigarette. He was wearing his best Italian suede trousers, an open-necked shirt with a cravat, and a hacking jacket. I could see why Selina had considered him devastating.

'I thought we'd go for a picnic,' he said.

'A picnic?' I looked doubtfully at the sky which was cloudy and a little threatening. 'Is that a good idea?'

He stuck the cigarette in the corner of his mouth and opened the passenger door for me, squinting his dark fringed eyes against the smoke. 'As I've actually been shopping for the food, it had better be.'

I studied him cautiously as he got into the driving seat and slammed the door. He didn't seem to be in an awfully good mood and I wondered what had annoyed him. We had had many a bitter battle in the past because of his uncertain temper, but I didn't feel like an argument today – after my first week at the training centre, I was too tired for one thing.

'What's the matter?' I asked him. 'Is everything all right?'

'Everything's fine,' he said shortly. 'I just don't feel like seeking company, that's all, and anyway, we've got to talk.'

This sounded unpromising, especially as he immediately pushed a Streisand cassette into the tape deck which made talking out of the question. He drove on, and I sat silently, as the cassette played and the throttle roared, and the main road became a side road, the side road became a lane, the lane became a cart-track, and the cart-track petered out on to a grassy bank beside a meandering stream sheltered by a copse of hazel trees, golden with catkins.

'Oh,' I said, delighted. 'It's lovely – how did you know it was here?'

Nick opened up the boot and pulled out picnic things which included two mohair day rugs with the initials MWH on the sides. 'I once had a girlfriend who lived in Crookham,' he said.

I flopped down on one of the rugs, feeling rather squashed. Nick had had a lot of girlfriends in the past, and if rumour was to be believed, not all of them had been single either. I watched him open a bottle of white wine with a practised hand, and accepted some in a plastic tumbler. He sat down on the rug and looked at me in an expectant manner.

'Well?' he said.

I looked at him in surprise. 'Well what?' I asked.

'Perhaps it would help if I gave you a clue,' he said. 'On my way over, I popped in to see the Fanes.'

'Oh, yes,' I said, 'and *was* she pretty?'

He looked at me for a moment as if he didn't know what I was talking about.

'The new girl,' I told him, 'you know, wonder woman.'

He frowned. 'No,' he said, and after some consideration, he added, 'she's tough, strong, efficient, and capable, but she isn't pretty.'

'I see,' I said. 'So she *is* as good as they said she was.' I stared down into my plastic tumbler and felt my heart drop several inches because I had believed the Fanes capable of exaggeration, and now I knew they had told the truth. 'What does the yard look like?' I asked him.

'The yard looks tidy, the cobbles are weeded, the boxes are properly mucked out, the horses are well strapped.' Nick regarded me steadily over the rim of his tumbler. 'She's worth every penny of fifty pounds a week.'

I didn't believe it. 'The Fanes aren't paying her that much,' I said incredulously, 'they couldn't afford it!'

'But it's the going rate for an experienced groom, isn't it?'

77

Nick asked in an even tone. 'After all, it's what you'll be getting.'

I took a sip of wine. 'I'd like to think so,' I said, 'but I'll bet you anything that the Fanes aren't paying her more than fifteen pounds a week, less probably.'

'Plus use of the horsebox, a room of her own, time off to compete, and keep of her own horse?'

'Has she got her own horse?' I said, nettled by the idea. 'They didn't say.'

'They said quite a lot to me,' Nick said, splashing more wine into his tumbler – the bottle was already half empty.

'Don't you think we should have something to eat?' I suggested. 'You're not supposed to drink and drive.'

'We'll eat when you've told me what you told the Fanes,' he said coldly, 'unless what Henrietta said was true and you didn't intend to tell anyone about where you are going after the course.'

With my mind still gnawing away miserably over the success of the new girl, I hardly heard what he said. I rolled over and looked into the stream. 'Tell me about the riding lessons and the grass liveries,' I said. After all, I thought, it's me she's replacing, I'm entitled to know.

The next minute I was hauled up into a sitting position by the neck of my good navy guernsey and Nick's furious face was next to my own. 'Tell me about *your* new job, Elaine,' he said in a dangerously quiet voice.

I stared at him, quite unable to speak.

'Or don't you want me to know?' he continued. 'Perhaps Henrietta was telling the truth for once, was she, when she said it was to be a secret?' He let go of my guernsey and turned away. 'You could have told me,' he said in disgust, 'you might have spared me having to hear it second-hand from the Fanes.'

I let out a sigh and put down my tumbler. Now I could see why he had been in such a bad mood, what all the dropped hints about wages and time off to compete had been leading up to. Trust the Fanes, I thought resentfully, to cast a blight even when they couldn't be present to do it in person.

'It isn't true,' I said. 'Honestly, Nick, I haven't got a job, not yet, I've only just sent off my advertisement.'

He turned back to me, scowling, not knowing whether to believe me or not.

'I haven't,' I assured him, 'I just couldn't bear the Fanes to think I hadn't got anything at all, when they were so cock-a-hoop over wonder woman, so I made it up. Anyway,' I added, 'you need money to advertise, and until they brought my wages, I hadn't any.'

This reminded me that I still owed him the petrol money and I searched through my pockets and presented him with it. He took it, but reluctantly. Now I had explained how things were, I knew that he believed me, but it was a little while before his humour was restored.

We lay on the hunt day rugs and stared into the stream.

'Now you've finally got away from the Fanes,' Nick told me, 'you have to steel yourself to forget them. They've found someone else to feel responsible for their equine cripples and to run their business, so you can put them behind you and set your sights on better things.'

'It would be a lot easier if the better things were already in sight,' I said, 'and if the Fanes didn't insist on having a stake in Legend.' Also, I thought rather miserably, it won't be easy to forget them. The Fanes, the unbearable, irritating, eccentric, irreplaceable Fanes, were going to leave a big gap in my life. We fell silent, thinking about the Fanes.

'Once,' said Nick, 'a horse and a chance to event were all you wanted.'

'And now,' I said, feeling desolate, 'it's all I've got.'

The first spot of rain fell upon the back of my neck. Nick immediately jumped to his feet and began to throw things into the boot of the car.

'I don't think we'll bother with the picnic, after all,' he said in a cheerful voice, 'I'll take you for tea in Crookham instead. I know the perfect place.'

I didn't doubt it.

9

Such An Excellent Store

The following week we were to ride the cross-country course as a whole for the first time. It was a testing course, consisting of twenty-nine fences up and down-hill, through water and woodland, and even though the chief had drilled us over the most awkward fences individually, we were all anxious about it by the time the day came. When Phillip, whose turn it was to cook, suggested a fried breakfast, we all groaned.

Phillip was visibly disappointed as, far from objecting to being included on the rota, he had actually been looking forward to showing off his talents as a chef. He contented himself with laying our beastly formica table with elaborate care, lining up the cereal packets and the bowls, putting out side plates, searching out saucers for our motley collection of mugs, scraping the marmalade into a basin, and decanting the milk into a jug; he even cut up the butter into neat little squares.

'Gordon Bennett,' Alice commented when she saw it, 'who's coming for breakfast, the Queen?'

Alice was not riding because The Talisman still had a puffy leg as a result of hitting the double. He was not actually lame, but the chief had decided he should do light work only until the leg was back to normal, and he had appointed Alice timekeeper and starter for the cross-country. She was not looking her best this morning, having finally been persuaded to see the nurse, who ran a mini-surgery in the yard two mornings a week to deal with bites, kicks, sprains, crushed toes, lice, ringworm, bumps on the head, and all the other minor ailments and accidents that working pupils and students were wont to suffer from. Nurse had issued Alice with some green acne ointment which made the spots look even more unsightly, and Alice, who didn't care what she looked like, made a point of plastering her face with it before every lesson to annoy the chief who, suspecting that she was being insubordinate, but unable to do very much about it, gave her some searching looks.

Selina appeared for breakfast, still in her track suit and running shoes, having managed to finish the morning run looking as immaculate as when she had started out. 'Well, this *is* an improvement, I must say,' she said. She settled herself at the table and looked round approvingly.

Mandy, flushed and wheezing, flopped into her chair with her Sony Walkman still in place, and Phillip, setting an evenly browned rack of toast in front of us, plucked the earphones off the top of her head in protest. If it had been anyone else, Mandy would have snatched them back, but as she was in love with Phillip, she switched it off and gave him a cow-eyed look of adoration.

Annemarie, whose table manners left a lot to be desired, threw herself into the vacant chair, grabbed a piece of Phillip's beautiful toast, piled three squares of butter on to it, flattened it with her knife, stirred her coffee with the blade and plunged it, still dripping, into the marmalade. Despite this appalling display, she still complained unceasingly about the quality of our accommodation, comparing it unfavourably with that of the Reitschule.

'I wasn't able to find a jamspoon,' Phillip apologized, 'sorry.'

Annemarie paused with a loaded toast inches from her mouth. 'There aren't any jam spoons to be found in this hole of a place,' she said with her customary disgust.

'And even if there were,' Selina pointed out, '*some* people might not know what they were for.'

One by one we got up from the table and went to get changed for the cross-country. I managed to be ready first and was sitting on Mandy's bed, having just negotiated the loan of a hairnet from Annemarie, when the door burst open and Selina appeared, looking furious.

'These breeches have *shrunk*!' she raged, her face white with temper. 'Lillywhites promised me *faithfully* they were pre-shrunk and machine washable!'

I had forgotten about the breeches, but now I saw with

dismay that the velcro fastenings only reached to her knees, and the waistband didn't meet at all. In retrospect, this was hardly surprising because my breeches were two sizes smaller than the ones they had replaced, but it had been a fact I had failed to consider in the anxiety of the moment.

There seemed nothing for it but to tell Selina what had happened. I opened my mouth to confess everything and offer to buy her a new pair of breeches, but she was not to be interrupted.

'I think it's utterly disgraceful,' she stormed. 'I shall create the most *almighty* scene, and what is more, I shall close my account!' She raced out of the cell, still wearing the breeches, to ring the store from the pay phone in the lecture hall.

Annemarie, who knew the story of the breeches, looked after her with vengeful satisfaction. 'Now there's going to be trouble,' she said, 'just you wait.'

I didn't have to wait long, Selina returned a few minutes later, looking serene.

'What did they say?' I breathed, trying hard not to sound over-anxious.

Selina smiled at the memory. 'Well, of course, they were *most* apologetic,' she said. 'I must admit to being positively warmed by their concern. They intend to take the matter up with the manufacturer, and naturally, they are sending an immediate replacement.'

'Well . . . naturally,' I said, 'I mean . . . why not?'

'I must say they are such an *excellent store*,' Selina went on in a self-congratulatory tone, 'but I am, after all, one of their most valued customers.' She sat down on the bed and peeled off the offending breeches and, after a moment of thoughtful hesitation, held them out to me. 'They should be just about your size now, Elaine,' she said in her sweetest voice, 'do please take them, and no . . .' she held up a restraining hand as my jaw fell open, 'please don't try to thank me, they are no earthly use to me, after all.' She rose from the bed, patted my shoulder in a queenly gesture, and went off in her lace-trimmed knickers to hunt out her second best.

I continued to sit on the bed with the breeches on my lap,

feeling stunned, but Annemarie folded up and fell across her bed in a paroxysm of helpless, hysterical laughter. I suppose that even at the Reitschule, it would have been considered a pretty good joke.

The chief stood by the Range Rover watching us work in our horses, beating an impatient tattoo on his boot as Alice sweated over a heap of papers on the tailboard, sorting out the draw for our starting order, and working out the times.

We were wearing our jerseys, our cross-country hats and safety harness, we had been given number cloths, and our stopwatches were strapped to our wrists. Our horses had studs screwed into their shoes to give them extra grip, their bandages were sewn on, their legs smeared with vaseline to assist them to slip instead of scrape over the fixed fences in the event of a mistake. All this made it as nerve-wracking as the real thing.

The chief supervised us individually as we gave our horses a sharp gallop to clear their wind, and sent us to Alice to collect our times, set to start at ten minute intervals. I had never given Legend his pipe-opener so close to starting before, and now I could see that it had been a mistake because he got excited and began to plunge about in an agony of impatience, knowing exactly what lay ahead and desperate to get on with it. I knew that event horses often became so wound up before the start of the cross-country phase that they jibbed out of sheer nerves at the last minute, napping, rearing and running backwards, losing valuable seconds after their starting time and often needing three people, one either side and one behind, to get them to approach the start at all. I didn't want Legend to get the habit, so I took him well away from Alice and her stopwatch, and with one eye on my times, written on my wrist with Viv's ballpoint, worked him steadily into a calmer frame of mind.

Viv and Balthazar went first, thundering away in a purposeful manner towards the first fence. Phillip set off ten minutes later, the roan horse's tail flying, and its white stockings flashing in the sunshine. Annemarie followed, looking tense and determined, and I was next.

83

As my starting time approached, I worked Legend nearer and nearer to Alice, slowing to a working trot and finally to a walk, so that as Alice began our count-down we were walking towards her, drew level, and cantered away on the exact second.

'Neat work, Elaine!' Alice bellowed, and Legend, realizing that we were off, gave a leap of joy.

It was a glorious morning, sunny and fresh, with a deep blue sky and a keen little breeze. The trees were coming into leaf, and the parkland over which the cross-country course was set was awash with a froth of white and yellow daffodils. The afternoon spent with Nick had helped me to resolve to put the Fanes and their affairs behind me, and to concentrate my energies exclusively towards Legend and my eventing career. The early morning running and the extra hours spent in the saddle were already having a beneficial effect on my health and fitness, and I felt confident and happy as we thudded across the turf. I was ready for anything.

Legend cleared the first fence easily, galloped over the tiger trap almost without noticing it, and had gained so much superfluous speed out of sheer *joie de vivre*, that I was forced to sit down hard in the saddle and fight to steady him as we flew downhill towards the telegraph pole in the middle of the shimmering lake. Showers of sparkling droplets flew into the air as we hit the water and cantered strongly towards the pole with more than enough impulsion to satisfy the chief, who was currently nowhere to be seen. Legend jumped the pole, landed with a tremendous splash, crossed the shallows in a succession of high-spirited leaps and bounds, gained the bank and pounded onwards towards the uphill double where The Talisman had cut his fetlock. As before, he cleared it easily, taking four effortless strides in between the fences and sailing cleanly out over the second part.

Things began to go awry after that because, perhaps made over-confident by past success, we took off too close to the brush where the Fanes had sheltered and scraped over the top in a hail of twigs, and followed this by making an appalling mess of the zig-zag rails.

There were four separate parts to the zig-zag, all set at different angles and varying distances and I somehow managed to misjudge Legend's stride and speed, placing him either too close or too far away from every rail, whilst he, calling upon every last ounce of athletic ability in his body, got over somehow, but not without a hammer blow to his front or hind shins each time, and a devastating peck on his final landing.

I didn't deserve to be still in the saddle by the end of it, but I was, just, and I struggled back over the pommel from halfway down his shoulder as he recovered his balance and trotted on, but with a peculiar, halting gait. I pulled him up and looked down, feeling sick with fright, to see what damage he had done to himself and saw the cause of it – yards of trailing bandage unwinding itself from his near fore; my stitching had come undone.

I jumped down to the ground, feeling shaken, and not helped by the fact that Legend was still eager to continue and was in no mood to stand still whilst I retrieved the lost bandage, repositioned the gamgee tissue, and wound up the crepe again, blessing the fact that I hadn't cut off the tapes and still had some method of securing it. Legend pranced and fidgeted as I fumbled with the tapes, knotting them several times for security, and the precious seconds ticked away. To make matters worse, a distant flash of reflected light told me that the chief was standing by the Range Rover with his binoculars trained upon us.

I cursed him as I clambered back into the saddle, knowing that I would be in deep trouble later and would probably have to spend hours sewing up bandages to prove I was capable of doing it properly. We cantered on. Legend, to my relief, appeared to be perfectly sound.

The next two fences, approached cautiously, with due regard to stride, speed, height and distance, we jumped clear, and now we entered a natural hollow, where a succession of narrow drop fences had been cut like giant steps out of the hillside. Perched on the very edge of each step was a timber jump made of railway sleepers, increasing in height as one descended and the steps themselves also widened on the descent, so that it needed a clever, scopey horse to negotiate it.

Legend, his bay head lowered to evaluate each step as it appeared below us, plummeted down the first, landed, rose again immediately over the first sleeper, plummeted again, took a stride, soared upwards, dropped down to land on the step below, took two strides, leapt, and as I struggled to remain in balance, dropped and landed safely at the bottom.

I clapped his neck as we cantered on, hoping that the chief had been watching our copybook descent. He hadn't, because when I looked up, I saw that he and Annemarie were engaged in energetic pursuit of the little part-bred Hanoverian who was playing a spirited game of catch-as-catch-can between the next two jumps. He had clearly deposited Annemarie, who had a grass stain on the seat of her breeches, at the steps which, because of his lack of scope, had become his personal bogey.

With a feeling of resignation, I reined in Legend and stopped my watch as Annemarie and the chief, both clearly infuriated, made alternate swoops at the little bay, and Selina appeared at the top of the steps to begin her descent. Mandy, I felt sure, would not be far behind and I knew that by this time Alice's timekeeping would be in a hopeless muddle and the chief would end the morning practically deranged with fury.

Selina appeared beside me, looking, I thought, rather pale after Flame Thrower's descent of the steps. She stopped her watch and observed the chase which was still going on ahead of us.

'Do you think we should assist?' she enquired.

'No,' I said, 'I don't think so.'

Selina watched the chief stalking the little bay, who with a guile born of many similar occasions, waited until he was within a hair's breadth of his rein before throwing up his head and trotting out of reach.

'No,' she said with a little smile, 'I don't think so, either.'

The door of the Duke of Newcastle opened and Phillip came in with the morning's post; an airmail letter from Germany for Annemarie, two typewritten envelopes for Selina, and a parcel for me, untidily wrapped, tied with orange baler twine, and addressed in Nigella's wandering hand.

Inside the parcel I found a vast, shapeless, blue jersey with red sleeves. Nigella had worn it when she had won a point-to-point in the days when we were shamelessly pot-hunting in aid of Legend's training fund. *It was lucky for me*, she had written, *so perhaps it will be lucky for you, Elaine*. I laid it on my bed and remembered when we had bought it from *Help the Aged* on Lady Jennifer's duty day. We had had to buy two jerseys, one blue and one red, and had cobbled the sleeves of one on to the other to achieve something like racing colours. It was hideous and so enormous that I could never wear it, but I was made to feel a little emotional by the thought which had prompted her to send it, especially as she had pinned to it the rest of the ten pound notes to make up the balance of my wages.

We wondered, Elaine, Nigella's letter continued, *if we could possibly come and see you on your next free afternoon. We really need to talk to you and hope you will agree* . . .

I could have refused. After all, I had decided to forget the Fanes completely and concentrate on my career. But, what difference will it make, I asked myself, to see them one last time? And suppose they've changed their minds and decided to relinquish their claim to a share in Legend? How much more satisfactory it would be to leave them on affectionate terms.

I went to find Selina and asked if I could borrow two of her envelopes.

She frowned. 'I will *give* you two envelopes, Elaine,' she said, 'because I hardly expect them to be returned, but if you are likely to require any more, you can buy perfectly good Basildon Bond at the village store.'

I took the envelopes, scribbled a note to Nigella telling them to come the following Monday afternoon, hunted out the garage bill, put it in the other envelope, and tucked three ten pound notes and three single pound notes in with it. Then I sealed them both. At least my side of the slate was clean. Now it was up to the Fanes.

10

Their Own Familiar Fields

Monday turned out to be rather dramatic, one way and another. Because the weather had been so perfect, we had all been for a long, blissfully leisured hack on Sunday evening, and so we spent part of the morning cleaning our tack. I went to collect the headcollars, which were kept in the yard store for convenience, and slipped over to the office to see if there was any post because I had been rather expecting a letter from Nick. Instead I got a short note from my father hoping I was enjoying the course, informing me that he would be coming to the junior trial with Lady Jennifer, and enclosing five pounds. He, at least, was confident that I would make the team.

I wandered through the car park, hung with headcollars, marvelling at the amount of correspondence Selina received every day, and stopped in my tracks to admire a beautiful pale green Rolls Royce, which crunched silently across the gravel and came to a halt just in front of me. A small, portly man in a dark suit and a silk tie emerged from the driver's seat.

'Hello,' he said in a cheerful voice, 'are you a student?'

I replied that I was and I wasn't, and I explained about the scholarship course.

'In that case,' he said, 'perhaps you would be kind enough to hunt out my daughter for me. I believe she's on the scholarship course as well.'

He smiled at me in an encouraging manner. He seemed very pleasant, very well-spoken; but possibly, I thought, a man of steel, a person not to be trifled with. I went.

I hadn't even asked who his daughter was, but I put together the authoritative manner and the Rolls Royce, and I concluded that the only scholarship student who could possible be his daughter was Selina.

I found her soaping the underside of her saddle, wearing a

88

pink nylon overall to protect her navy blue track suit. She looked surprised when I said her father was waiting to see her.

'I thought he was in Montreal this week,' she said in a perplexed tone, as she removed her overall, patted her already immaculate hair, and followed me out into the yard. She looked even more surprised when they came face to face. Her visitor looked rather taken aback as well.

Selina opened her eyes wide with astonishment. 'Why,' she exclaimed, 'it's Mr Tintoft, isn't it?' She turned to me looking rather distressed. 'This isn't my father, Elaine, it's Mr Tintoft, head of the departmental stores.'

There didn't seem anything I could say to this. I just stared at them both and wondered what was happening.

Mr Tintoft was staring at Selina with an outraged expression on his face. 'And you, young lady, are Jane Lejeune, unless I am very much mistaken,' he said in a furious voice. 'You and I already have one score to settle, and now look set for another, if you are here for the purpose I suspect.'

Selina summoned up her most imperious manner and held up a restraining hand. 'Mr Tintoft, I think you are mistaking me for someone else,' she said firmly. 'I don't actually know you at all, we have never been introduced, and I only recognized your face from the newspapers.'

'And I recognize *your* face from the newspapers,' Mr Tintoft retorted in a heated voice, 'and if you've come here, sailing under false colours, the way you sailed into my stores . . .'

'I can assure you, Mr Tintoft,' Selina cut in sharply, 'that you are totally mistaken, *totally*,' she emphasized, 'and if you imagine that my being here has anything at all to do with your daughter, I can assure you again, that it is *positively* untrue.' She turned to me for confirmation. 'Elaine,' she commanded, 'tell Mr Tintoft who I am.'

'Selina,' I told him, 'Selina Gibbons.'

'And why am I here?'

'Training for eventing,' I said, 'trying for a place at the junior trial.'

Mr Tintoft stifled a bark of incredulous laughter. 'And just how old is a junior these days?' he enquired.

'Under twenty-one,' Selina said, and the corners of her mouth quivered.

Mr Tintoft stared at her for a moment and then his shoulders began to shake with supressed mirth. He turned to me, still standing beside them, taking it all in and not understanding a word. 'I think, if you wouldn't mind, you had better fetch me Vivienne,' he said.

I left them giggling together like a couple of first-formers and went to find Viv. She was soaping a bridle in the tackroom. Her dungarees were splashed with water and there was a smear of glycerine saddle soap across her cheek.

'Viv', I said, 'your father's here.'

She stared at me and her face went very pale. 'What for?' she whispered. 'What does he want?'

'I don't know,' I said helplessly, 'I expect he'll tell you that.'

She dropped the whole bridle into the scum-covered water and it hit the bottom with a dismal clunk. 'Hell, Elaine,' she said, 'oh *hell*.' She sounded as if she might burst into tears.

There was nothing I could do or say, but: 'Oh, *Viv*,' I said, remembering, 'you said he sold sandals along the Mile End Road.'

She looked up at me, tight-lipped. 'So it's Knightsbridge,' she said, 'what's the difference?'

'There's a lot of difference,' I said.

She looked down at the scummy water and then unexpectedly spat into it. 'Well, you can stuff the bloody difference,' she snapped viciously and, racing off out of the tack room, she slammed the door so hard that a tin of louse powder jumped off the shelf.

Viv didn't appear for lunch, she stayed in her cell with her transistor turned on full blast. Selina's expression didn't encourage questions and I didn't ask any. Mandy was the only other person present, but as she had her life support machine clamped over her ears, she was not much company. I felt rather glad that the Fanes were coming because at least I would have someone to talk to.

Henrietta and Nigella arrived at three, looking fearsome.

Nigella wore a calf-length cotton skirt whose hem dipped everywhere and a yellowing shawl with a long fringe which might have been cashmere and once very fine, but now was just dubious. Henrietta wore Nigella's mohair jersey, her own purple mini-skirt which showed a lot of thigh clad in mustard yellow tights, and her terrible leg warmers. Their wild and beautiful hair looked as though it hadn't been combed for a week, although Nigella had made some attempt to tidy hers by securing it at the back of her neck with a bucked D-piece from the bit rings of a pelham bridle.

We paid a courtesy call on Legend, and then walked through the park, admiring the daffodils, with the sun warming our backs. The Fanes seemed subdued and I guessed that something was troubling them. I knew that they would only tell me about it in their own time and so we talked about the course and the other students, and how Legend was performing, and what I thought our chances were of getting into the team for the junior trial.

'And what about you,' I said eventually, 'how's the new girl?'

There was a pause, during which we stopped walking and Henrietta removed one of her scuffed, pink stiletto-heeled shoes in order to examine the heel, which had worn down far below its tip.

'The thing is,' Nigella said in an uncomfortable voice, 'that we're in rather deep trouble at the moment.'

'It's true, Elaine, honestly,' Henrietta added as if, for some reason, I might disbelieve it. She replaced her shoe, and as in all moments of stress, fell to picking at the cuff of the mohair jersey.

'What sort of trouble?' I asked.

'Oh,' Nigella said, a note of inevitability in her voice, 'it's *financial*.'

'Yes,' I agreed, 'I suppose it would be.' After all, every one of their problems stemmed from lack of finance, one way or another.

'The rats have eaten the electricity cables,' Henrietta said.

'What did you say?' I looked at her in astonishment. Whatever I had expected, it certainly wasn't this.

'They've eaten the electricity cables, gnawed off the plastic coating. Rats do, apparently,' Nigella said.

'So we've no electricity,' Henrietta said, her pride forcing her to add, 'but we've got candles, and the Aga, naturally.'

'Oh,' I said, 'naturally.' I imagined them sitting at the kitchen table in the candlelight, walking up the cold, dusty staircase by the light of a single, flickering, flame.

'We've had the electricity people in, and we've got to have the whole place rewired,' Nigella said, 'it's going to cost two thousand pounds.'

'Goodness,' I said, it sounded an enormous amount. 'Have you got it?'

'No,' Nigella said.

'What about the bank,' I suggested, 'won't they help?'

'Mummy went to see them, of course,' Henrietta said, 'but they consider they've helped us enough. We already owe them quite a lot, they're threatening to foreclose.'

I wondered how much they owed the bank, hundreds? thousands? As if by mutual consent, we all sat down on the grass.

'They want us to sell,' Nigella said, 'in fact, it's rather worse – they're going to force us to sell.'

This was terrible news. 'But what about your business?' I asked them. 'What about your new girl? Your improved prospects?'

'We haven't got a new girl anymore.' Nigella kept her eyes on her shoes, the red tap-dancing shoes with the scraped sides that she regarded as her best. 'She's left.'

'*Left*?'

'She turned out not to be suitable after all,' Nigella said. 'There were . . . difficulties.'

'Difficulties?'

'She wanted more than we could afford to pay,' Henrietta burst out, 'and she complained all the time, about the room, about the food, about there not being any hot water, and then . . .' she tailed off.

'And then?'

'And then the lights went out,' Nigella said.

I could have laughed, it sounded so ridiculous, and so very

typical of the Fanes, but I could see that it was also tragic. 'If you sell,' I asked them, 'what will happen to your business?'

'The business will have to close,' Nigella said, 'after all, it's the land which will bring in the money to repay the bank – the house isn't worth anything, it's practically a ruin.'

It was the first time I had heard her admit it. 'But the horses,' I said, 'what about the horses?'

'We'll sell them wherever possible,' she said 'and those we can't sell we'll have put down. That way, at least the kennels will benefit.' She looked up at me, knowing that I would take this badly. 'There isn't really any future for some of them,' she said, 'and at least they won't be shipped on the hoof or anything awful like that. They're put down kindly in their own familiar fields. They don't know, after all, what's going on.'

I had known the answer even before I had asked, but now I thought of Nelson with his stitched up eye socket and his threadbare coat, of the bad-tempered chestnut whom nobody loved, of the black horse who never stood still, and of the beautiful bay mare who was never sound for more than a few months at a time. My heart gave a frightening lurch as I realized how it would end for them, and I knew that I should never be able to bear it. 'We can't let it happen,' I said, 'there must be some way, there must be *something* we can do.'

'Well, yes,' Nigella said, 'there is *something*.' She began to twist the end of her ghastly shawl and she looked embarrassed. 'The thing is, Elaine,' she began, 'we know how awkward it would be for you to come back now, and by now, I mean after the trial, especially with your new job prospects and everything . . .'

'And we couldn't pay you fifty pounds a week,' Henrietta put in almost sharply, 'so there would be no point in promising it.'

'But if you would consider coming back to us,' Nigella said, 'we think things might possibly be all right.'

I looked at them in despair. I was incredibly touched by their naive belief that my expertise would have such a beneficial effect on their business that they would be able to surmount even these new and totally impossible difficulties. But for the life of me I couldn't see how I could earn two thousand pounds immediately. I could continue with the grass liveries and the riding lessons, we could break and school horses, and perhaps we could still make our own hay for the winter, but none of this would bring in money quickly, or in sufficient quantity, to satisfy the bank.

'Nigella,' I said, 'how will my coming back make any difference?'

Nigella seemed reluctant to answer this, and so it was Henrietta who replied.

'If you come back,' she said, instantly more cheerful, 'we can sell Legend. You can buy another cheap, unschooled youngster to replace him, we can pay our bills, and then we can start all over again.'

Even knowing Henrietta as well as I did, I couldn't believe she had said it. 'Sell *Legend*?' I said, appalled.

'Well, why not?' she wanted to know. 'He'll be worth a bomb after all this intensive training, especially if he gets picked for the Junior Olympics. We'll get twenty thousand for him at least, it's a *fortune*.' It seemed to her to be the perfect solution and she looked at me expectantly. 'What do you think?'

I lay flat out on the grass, feeling absolutely stunned. The Fanes had offered me the chance to go back; they actually *wanted* me to go back, but they had made sure I could never accept by expecting me to sacrifice Legend. Yet, if I didn't go back, the hirelings would be sold – or slaughtered. Whichever way I looked at it, the situation was equally horrendous.

'I think I've been hit by a sledgehammer,' I said.

11
Hard Going

Halt at X, rein back four steps, proceed at working trot (sitting) . . . I squeezed Legend into a trot, and fixed my eyes beyond the end marker in order to keep him absolutely straight.

'Stop!' the chief shouted. 'Stop and begin again, Miss Elliot, and this time I want to see a more fluent rein back, counting, if you must, one-two-three-four, not one-two-three-and-a-half!'

I took Legend back to X, halted, counted four whole strides back, squeezed him again into trot, and this time I got as far as E.

'Stop!' commanded the chief. 'Circle at E, Miss Elliot, means circle at E, not just before E, and not just after E. Accuracy, obedience and control are the essence of dressage; do it again please!'

We did it again, and again, before the chief professed himself satisfied. We repeated our halts, our leg-yielding, our transitions, and our turns-on-the-forehand so many times that my head began to spin and I felt panic rising in my chest. Legend, sensing it, stiffened into resistance, and the chief, raising his eyes to the heavens in a supplicatory gesture, finally waved us out and called in the next student.

Three weeks into the course, the work somehow seemed harder instead of easier. I was sure that I was putting maximum effort into my work and still it didn't seem to be enough to please the chief, who constantly stopped and corrected me, making me ask Legend to repeat movements and jump fences time after time, even when I felt sure our performance had equalled that of the other students.

I rode away from the arena, took Legend into the shade and dismounted, running up the irons and loosening his girth. With the team due to be announced at the end of the week, I felt sure we hadn't a chance of being chosen, and if we weren't, I knew that the fault would be mine and not Legend's. I've been too long without formal instruction, I thought, and in the time I have been with the Fanes my riding must have deteriorated badly without my realizing it.

I watched Phillip perform a fluent rein back into sitting trot under the now approving eye of the chief, and turned away, not wanting to see. Legend nudged my pockets hopefully and I found him a peppermint. He found it difficult to eat, rolling it round in his mouth and getting it mixed up with the bits of his double bridle, an expression of deep concentration on his face. If I sold you, I thought, if I found a good home for you, a family home, a comfortable well-off home, with someone to love you as much as I do, somebody who is a better rider than I am, would you really mind? Would you even notice?

I leaned my head on his silken neck, sick to my heart.

The next morning had been set aside for show-jumping practice. The fences in the paddock were not high, in fact hardly any of them exceeded three feet six inches, and they were also set at a good distance apart. Although there were spreads, uprights, combination fences, and the course included a water jump and a change of direction, it was still a far cry from the high, angled close-set fences of the professional show-jumping arena.

The chief had continually stressed the importance of the show-jumping phase, and warned us again and again against being over confident or ill-prepared, because easy as it may look, a fence down in the show-jumping could lose us a close-fought competition. At the junior trial, the show-jumping would be phase two, following on after the dressage tests and coming before the cross-country. This set us rather a different problem from the three-day event proper, where it came at the end of everything, after the dressage, the roads and tracks, the steeplechase, and the cross-country, when the show-jumping phase was designed, not as further punishment for a horse and rider already tested to the limit of their endurance, but as an exercise to prove that they were still fit and supple enough to jump an accurate, intelligent round. Then, it was full of pitfalls for the tired or complacent horse and rider, but at the junior trial our horses would be fit, fresh, and bursting for action. We had to gauge their pre-ring preparation exactly right. They needed to be sober and obedient enough to go in and jump a clear round, but not having had their sparkle blunted for the cross-country.

Due to the dry, sunny weather, the ground was already baked and hard, and all of our horses wore support bandages, tendon boots and over-reach boots as we rode into the jumping paddock, where the fences sparkled, white, green, red and blue in the sunshine. The chief, still wearing his long boots and his jacket, although as a concession to the unseasonably hot weather he had exchanged his tweed cap for a straw trilby, positioned himself inside the marked off arena with his stopwatch and a starting bell.

Annemarie went first. She achieved what was so very nearly a clear round due to a brilliant display of precision riding marred only by the bay tipping a pole off the triple spread.

'If she'd let him crack on a bit at that and really stretch out his neck, he might have managed it,' Viv grumbled. 'Still, I'm glad he didn't.' She had never offered me any information on what had happened when her father had arrived, and I had never asked, knowing that if she had wanted to discuss it, she would have done so.

We watched Alice and The Talisman go round the course, rattling every fence but, by a miracle, not knocking down a single pole. Although it looked awful, and sounded worse, this was quite a feat on Alice's part, as The Talisman had little or no respect for coloured poles, knowing perfectly well he could plough through them without the slightest injury to himself if he chose. Theirs was not a copybook round, but it was exciting and, as The Talisman cantered out of the arena with his hooves scarred with paint, we heaved sighs of relief.

Mandy and Fox Me went next, sailing round in their usual magical manner; their perfect understanding and the pretty bay horse's undoubted courage and exceptional ability stood them in good stead both across country and in the show-jumping arena.

Phillip and the roan horse also achieved a clear round and so did Selina and Flame Thrower, the latter combination jumping each fence in a neat, methodical manner, as if they had been doing it for years. Viv and Balthazar looked fit to make it four in a row until the powerful chestnut ran out at the last part of the triple combination, earning Viv a verbal lashing from the chief. She took Balthazar at it again, sullen faced, and this time they jumped it perfectly.

It was my turn. I had walked the course previously and worked out speed, stride and distance for every combination, noted the approach, groundline, height and spread of every fence. I was determined that we should jump clear and we did. Legend soared over the fences, clearing them with inches to spare, making nothing of them at all. Even the chief found nothing to complain about.

'Very good, Miss Elliot,' he said as we cantered through the finish.

As we trotted across to the others, I leaned over and slapped Legend's neck, feeling a surge of relief and renewed confidence. Perhaps this was the turning point, perhaps there would be a place for us in the team after all. Surely, I told myself, I would be a fool to consider giving up Legend now, surely nothing, not even the Fanes, would be worthy of such a sacrifice?

Getting a grip on my emotions and my common sense for the first time since the Fanes had spilled out their devastating news, I suddenly found I could think positively again. I felt sure there was no need to have the hirelings shot. Why not offer them free to approved homes, so that they could live out their remaining years peacefully in semi-retirement? I knew that *Horse & Hound* was always full of advertisements from people of limited means who had the facilities but not the ready cash. *Companion wanted for youngstock* – that would do for the black horse; *Bombproof elderly hack, about 15hh wanted by gentlewoman with back complaint* – that would suit Nelson perfectly; nothing I had seen sprang readily to mind as suitable for the bad-tempered chestnut, but I was sure we would be able to place them all eventually. We might even advertise them ourselves, with a brief description of each. Why, I would even draft and pay for the advertisement myself. I didn't see how it could fail.

Fired by such thoughts, I turned my attention to the problem of the Fanes themselves. Wouldn't they be better suited in a smaller place anyway, somewhere more economic and easier to run than Havers Hall? In my imagination I saw them installed in a comfortable three-bedroom cottage with full central heating and a fashionably coloured suite in the bathroom. It all seemed so terribly simple and obvious that I was amazed it hadn't occurred to me before.

'Letter for you, Elaine.'

Phillip dropped the familiar, crested envelope on to my plate. He looked exhausted and, looking round the table, I saw that everyone did. Viv looked pale and no longer bothered to apply her makeup. Alice, despite liberal applications of green acne ointment, had broken out in a fresh rash of spots across her chin and forehead. Mandy had dark shadows of fatigue under her eyes and a cold sore on her lip. Annemarie was tense and bad-tempered, and even in repose her square face was set like a piece of granite. Only Selina appeared unaffected by the general tension now that selection was just three days away; sailing graciously through it all, confident probably, that her rightful place in the team was totally secure.

The letter was from Lady Jennifer, written in a spidery hand below the Fane crest.

My Dear Elaine, (she had written)
The girls have told me about their plans to resolve our little difficulty, and I am writing to say that I would not dream of asking you to part with Legend, in fact I positively forbid you even to consider it. It was frightfully thoughtless and unfair of them ever to suggest such a thing – you must forget it entirely and concentrate your energies on getting into the team for the junior trial – we will all be there to support you!
You must promise me you will not waste even a second worrying about what I am sure is only a temporary setback; the bank have been

terribly understanding in allowing us a fortnight's grace before any decision is made and one is always so incredibly optimistic that everything will turn out all right.

   Good Luck!
    and lots of love
     Jennifer Fane

My heart warmed towards Lady Jennifer as I read the letter. It was so typical of her to make little of their problems in order that I should be able to concentrate on the course. Well, I wouldn't let her down. If it was within my capabilities to get into the team, I would do it. I would also take her advice and postpone any further action on the implementation of my plans for the rescue of the hirelings and for the future comfort of the Fanes themselves until after the junior trial.

A fortnight would give me all the time I needed.

Due to the hard going there was to be no cross-country practice that afternoon, but a lesson in the indoor school instead. We were all husbanding our horses' legs carefully, knowing that a sprain, or concussion on the iron ground could put us out of the team.

I took Legend into one of the tan surfaced lunging rings to give him some gentle work on both reins in lieu of the morning's work he was going to miss, and he trotted round, flexing his neck and reaching for the bit, swishing his silky black tail. Despite the injuries he had suffered in a horrendous road accident the previous year, I was pleased and relieved to see that he was as sound and level as ever.

After the lunging, I replaced Legend's bridle, roller, and side-reins with a headcollar and took him out to graze from the end of a rope. He had been used to long periods of freedom in the park at Havers Hall, and even in the winter I had turned him out in a New Zealand rug for a few hours two or three times a week to encourage him to relax and to keep his temper sweet.

I had noticed some particularly long, succulent grass growing in the shade of a copse at the end of the show-jumping paddock, and I took him there. Legend tore great mouthfuls out by the roots, and I watched him idly, glad of a little relaxation myself, listening to the satisfying sound of his champing jaws. I started to think about the Fanes, remembered Lady Jennifer's instructions, and thought about Nick instead.

I didn't expect to see him again before the junior trial because they were in the middle of whelping at the kennels and he was taking a draft of experienced, older hounds, to a hunt in the north on Monday, and was expecting to be away for a few days. He had made me promise to ring him though, on Saturday, as soon as the names of the team had been announced. Good or bad, he had insisted, and good or bad I had promised.

Thinking about all this, I gradually became aware of approaching voices, angry voices, on the other side of the copse, and as they got nearer, I recognized them as belonging to Annemarie and Viv who had met up while hacking in the park.

'Your horse stopped at the combination,' Annemarie was saying in a scornful voice, 'at least my horse doesn't *refuse*. You don't get anywhere in eventing if your horse is a coward.'

'Balthazar didn't stop,' Viv said in a furious voice, 'he ran out. He ran out because *I* let him run out, it was *my* fault. Your horse knocked the last rail off the triple because he couldn't make the spread, he may never *refuse*, but he still can't do it, he hasn't got the scope. Balthazar *can* do it, he's physically capable of it. Your horse isn't and that's what counts in eventing!'

In the silence which followed I held my breath.

'What did you say?' Annemarie asked in a hard little voice.

'I said,' Viv repeated with a weary sigh, obviously already wishing she hadn't, 'that your horse can't cope with spreads. He tries, he's bold enough, and brave enough, but he just hasn't got the reach. Bloody hell, Annemarie, you ride him, you ought to *know*.'

'No,' Annemarie shouted, 'I don't know! You're wrong! He can do it, he *can*, and I'll prove it! I'll show you!'

There was all of a sudden a scattering of gravel from the drive which bordered the paddock, and Annemarie and her little bay hurled through the gap and charged towards the marked out arena with its painted fences. Annemarie's hat, which she must have removed because of the heat, bounced away across the grass like a rugby ball.

'Come back, you fool!' Viv yelled in an agonized voice. 'You know you're not allowed to jump without supervision, you haven't got your hat on either!'

But Annemarie was not listening. I watched, horrified, as she steered her horse towards the triple, minus support bandages, minus even a preliminary balancing canter, and pushed him hard at it with her legs. Any other horse would have refused, point blank, to tackle it, but the little bay part-bred Hanoverian, trained to a high standard of discipline by the Reitschule, summoned his lion-like courage, steadied, lengthened, gathered himself, took off, and powered by his own determination and Annemarie's willpower, flew upwards and cleared the poles. Then he landed with a sickeningly jarring impact on his front legs, buckled to his knees, and sent Annemarie hurtling over his ears, to land head-first on the baked, iron-hard ground.

The little bay horse managed to struggle to his feet, but Annemarie didn't. She just lay where she had landed as Viv on Balthazar, and I, dropping Legend's headcollar rope, tore across the parched grass towards her.

12

Questions and Answers

I stayed, staring helplessly down at Annemarie, whilst Viv galloped to the yards to bring assistance. I tried desperately to remember the first aid I had learned for my Horsemaster's Certificate but all I could think of was that I should loosen any tight clothing, especially at the neck. I couldn't get to Annemarie's neck because she was lying face downwards and I dared not try to move her. I was sure she must be dead and I felt sick at the thought; sick and dizzy and very, very frightened.

The chief's Range Rover had arrived and he was pulling a stretcher out of the back, when suddenly, terrifyingly Annemarie rose from the ground into a sitting position and stared at me. 'What happened?' she demanded.

'Lie down at once, Miss Maddox,' the chief barked, 'you must remain perfectly still.'

Annemarie lay down again obediently with her boots together and her hands pressed to her sides like a toy soldier. 'Where's my horse,' she hissed to me, 'is he all right?'

I didn't want to answer this, because I knew perfectly well that he wasn't all right. 'He's with Legend,' I said, 'he hasn't gone far. I'll catch him in a minute.'

Annemarie nodded, satisfied. The chief, helped by an ashen-faced Viv, rolled her gently on to the stretcher. While they were doing so, I ran to pick up Annemarie's hat and laid it on her chest, like a crusader's shield, hoping that the chief would just think it had fallen off before she hit the ground. She would be in trouble, I knew, for jumping without supervision, and there would be punishment enough when she saw what had happened to her little bay horse, because I realized, as I walked towards the two horses in the shade of the copse, that something heartbreakingly awful had happened to him when he had landed.

Legend was still pulling grass greedily, but the little bay was just standing with his head lowered, patches of sweat forming on his neck, his nose pinched with pain, and his two front legs already beginning to fill. I had been afraid that he might have broken something, but as I picked up the end of his broken rein and took Legend by his halter rope, the brave little horse moved forward slowly and reluctantly. Together we made painful progress into the yard and I was able to shout to one of the working pupils to go and ask reception to call out the vet as an emergency.

While Annemarie was transported to hospital to have her head X-rayed for possible skull fracture, the vet was in the stable with her horse; feeling, probing, injecting with anti-inflammatory and pain-killing drugs, and giving instructions for the use of diuretics, cold pressure bandages on the injured legs and support bandages on the hind legs. Extra thick bedding was laid, an extra blanket was provided, and at the end of it the little bay stood with bulky dressings strapped to his front legs, trying to rest one after the other, too uncomfortable to attempt to lie down, his mash untouched, his hay net ignored. There was nothing broken, the vet said, nothing that time wouldn't heal, and in six months, eight perhaps, or ten, he would be almost as good as new. Of course, tendons which had been so badly sprained might never be quite as strong again, but with careful treatment there was no reason why he shouldn't make a full recovery, provided that one faced the fact that he was unlikely to event again.

Viv had gone to the hospital with Annemarie and I stayed in the yard at lunchtime, unable to face the inquests and speculation I knew would be taking place inside the Duke of Newcastle. I strapped away gloomily at Legend as he pulled at his haynet and for the first time since I had first set my heart on an eventing career, I considered the moral aspect of testing a horse to the limits of its ability, when the consequences could be something like this – or even worse.

I knew that Annemarie had done a stupid thing out of anger, hurt pride and deep, burning ambition, and I was sure that in the same situation, I wouldn't have reacted in the same way. and yet, goaded almost beyond endurance, could I be *that* sure? I realized that we were still only on the bottom rung of the eventing ladder, and that further up, the wastage in horses was high; they broke their bones, their tendons were irreparably ruptured, their hearts gave out. It was all very well for a human athlete to test his own abilities almost to breaking point, but was it fair to form a partnership where one half of the combination had no voice and had no way of saying, 'stop now, I've had enough.'

Troubled by these and similar thoughts, I went to look again at the little bay horse with his hugely swollen, hot, painful legs, and his heart-wrenchingly miserable expression, and I felt a hopeless anger because there was nothing I could do. There was not a glimmer of hope, not a crumb of comfort that I could offer. And I knew that the pathetic creature I was looking at could have been any horse, it could have been my horse, and unless I was very, very fortunate, one day it would be.

After the initial shock of Annemarie's accident had worn off, the other scholarship students soon recovered their spirits, but I didn't, and Viv was still upset by what had happened as we set off round the perimeter of the cross-country course on our early morning run the following day.

'What will happen to Annemarie?' I wondered. 'Will they send her home?' By a miracle, the X-rays had shown no injury to her skull at all, although the hospital had insisted on keeping her for a few days under observation. She was, as Viv said ruefully, and not without a touch of reluctant admiration, a tough nut in more ways than one.

'How can they send her home?' Viv said. 'She'd have to go back to Germany, and what would happen to her horse then? He's not fit to travel anywhere. No, the chief will have to keep her here. He'll probably end up giving her a job on one of the yards.'

'She won't think much of that,' I said, 'not after the Reitschule.'

Viv allowed herself a little grin as we pounded around the

lake and began to run up the rise. 'I doubt if we'll hear very much about the Reitschule in future.'

'But we'll never hear the last about her losing her place in the team,' I panted. Annemarie had not yet been told how severely her horse was injured, and we all knew what a devastating shock it would be for her. None of us were looking forward to the day she came back from hospital.

'I wouldn't lose any sleep over it,' Viv told me, 'she might still get to ride in the team after all.'

I looked at her in astonishment as we laboured up to the top of the rise. 'How?' I gasped.

Viv made no reply to this. She just patted the side of her nose in an admonitory gesture and, gaining her second wind, sprinted off down the hill.

The following morning I received the first replies to my advertisement. I took them into the bathroom and locked the door in order to gain some privacy because Selina was in the bedroom, doing some surprisingly early typing.

Two of the letters I tore up at once and flushed down the lavatory; the first being from a small suburban riding school who offered keep for my own horse – *we presume he lives out*, they said, and caravan accommodation, plus a wage of eight pounds and fifty pence for a six-day week. The hours were 8A.M. until 8P.M., with an hour for lunch and two ten-minute coffee breaks.

The second was from an active, retired gentleman who required an attractive and lively female companion for horse-related activities – photograph essential. I dismissed this as being highly suspect.

The third letter I just couldn't believe. It was the perfect solution to all my problems. It offered a wage of fifty pounds a week, plus accommodation for my own horse, use of a cross-country course, indoor school and BSJA regulation jumps for training purposes, a horsebox was available if required, time off for competitions was negotiable, hostel accommodation would be provided for myself (with other staff), and I could start whenever suitably convenient. I didn't even have to attend for an interview.

I sat on the side of the bath feeling rather shaken. I had been worried that nothing would come of the advertisement, that at the end of the course, there would be no prospect in view. If this had happened, I would have had to turn Legend away for the summer, paying rent for grazing, whilst I found other work, as a shop-assistant perhaps, or a waitress; that, or sell Legend and go back to the Fanes, either of which would have made me exceedingly miserable.

But the more I looked at the letter, beautifully typewritten on headed notepaper with the logos of the BHS and the ABRS on either side, the more worried I became. In the end I had almost convinced myself that it wasn't genuine; that someone had played an unkind practical joke; that it was altogether too perfect a solution to be true.

There was only one thing to be done. I had to go and find out.

I unlocked the bathroom door, ran out of the back door of the Duke of Newcastle, past the steaming muckheaps, across the yards, dodging horses, pupils, and staff, and arrived, panting, at the office. I opened the door.

The chief regarded me with irritation from behind his desk. 'There is a notice outside requesting people to knock before entering,' he snapped, 'this is a private office, Miss Elliot, not a public right of way.'

'And I want to be sure that this is a genuine letter,' I said, 'not just someone's idea of a joke.' I placed the reply to my advertisement on top of his memorandum pad.

He looked at it. 'Ah,' he said. 'That.'

'So you do know about it,' I asked him, 'you have seen it before?'

'Of course I've seen it before,' the chief looked at me as if I might easily be out of my mind. 'I wrote it.' He pointed to the signature. 'I even signed it, but if you still doubt it, I can show you the copy.'

'I don't want to see the copy,' I said hastily, 'I just want to know if you are serious. Do you really mean it?'

'Of course I mean it,' he barked, 'why else would I have written it?'

I sat down abruptly on the little wooden chair. 'But how

did you know it was me?' I asked him, 'when I advertised under a box number?'

'Miss Elliot,' the chief said patiently, 'there is a system in existence which has evolved in order to prevent embarrassment to both parties when an advertisement carries a box number. Normally you place your reply in an outer envelope listing the people to whom your reply should not be forwarded. In your case I listed the only person to whom my reply *should* be forwarded.'

I stared at him, impressed. 'But how did you know I was going to advertise anyway?'

He sighed. 'Haven't you realized yet, how quickly word travels? Your friend Nicholas Forster is a good friend of Mr Felix Hissey, who is sponsoring your scholarship course, and is in constant touch with me to keep abreast of your progress.'

'*My* progress?'

'Not just *your* progress, Miss Elliot,' the chief said impatiently, 'everyone's progress.'

'Well, yes,' I said, 'of course, but I still don't really understand why you should want me to work here, unless you're offering me a job out of the kindness of your heart, out of charity, because you know I'm in a difficult position.'

'I don't offer people jobs out of the kindness of my heart,' the chief snapped, 'only if I consider I can put their talents to good use.'

'But what talents have I got?' I wondered. 'I'm not trained to teach, and I know you don't think much of my riding ability.'

The chief threw up his chin in an enquiring manner. 'What makes you think that, Miss Elliot?'

'Because you're always picking on me during instruction,' I said, 'making me repeat things, because I never seem to be able to please you.'

The chief rested his chin in his hands and regarded me thoughtfully. 'Has it never occurred to you that I might be spending more time on you because you are the most promising student on the course?' he said.

I couldn't believe it. 'No,' I said, 'no, *never*.'

'Good,' he said in a satisfied voice. He handed me the reply to my advertisement. 'You may be needing this. You may be requiring to reply to it.'

'Yes,' I said with conviction, 'I shall certainly need to reply.'

'If your reply is in the affirmative, Miss Elliot,' said the chief, eyeing me sternly, 'you will be required to train for Assistant Instructor's Certificate and progress upwards until you hold a full BHSI qualification. You could then specialize in preparing students for three-day eventing, if you so desired.'

'I suppose I could,' I said, 'if I so desired.'

'And do you so desire?' the chief wanted to know.

'I don't know,' I said, 'I've never even considered it.'

'Then go away, Miss Elliot,' he commanded. 'Consider it.'

I got up from the chair. There was one last question I wanted to ask. 'Why did you go to the trouble of answering my advertisement, when you could have just called me into the office and offered me the job face to face?'

The chief looked up at me and he very nearly smiled. 'I like to have everything in writing, Miss Elliot,' he said, 'efficient, orderly documentation is the key to the smooth running of every establishment.'

I was suddenly overwhelmed with gratitude and affection for this brusque, far-seeing, kind-hearted man. 'Oh!' I exclaimed, 'I'm so *terribly* grateful.'

He picked up a few papers, as if they had suddenly demanded his instant attention.

'Be sure to close the door on your way out, Miss Elliot,' he said.

13

Selection Day

We filed into the lecture hall on selection day, feeling tense. Annemarie was not with us. The chief had broken the news to her as gently as he was able and, as we had known she would, she had taken it very badly. She had stayed on her bed with her face to the wall, refusing to eat or to speak for a day and a night, after which she had got up and taken over the nursing of her little bay horse with justifiably contrite devotion. Everyone agreed that Annemarie had needed a lesson, but in paying the price of blind ambition, it had been tragic that her horse had suffered most.

The chief was already installed behind the lecture stand when we arrived, straightening his papers impatiently. 'Hat off, Mr Hastings,' he snapped, as Phillip took his seat wearing the sailcloth cap he habitually wore in front of the chief, 'this is a team selection announcement, not *La Tour de France*.'

Phillip removed his cap somewhat reluctantly to reveal his platinum forelock, now showing quarter of an inch of dark regrowth. The chief threw up his chin in a startled manner, leaned forward to ascertain that it wasn't a trick, or a wig, and decided to ignore it. He rustled his papers officiously. 'Hrmmmm,' he said

I took my seat feeling reasonably confident. After my interview with the chief, I fully expected to be included in the team, together with Phillip and Selina, whom I considered to be the other two certainties. As to who would make up the rest of the team, I honestly didn't know.

Mandy and Fox Me were incredibly consistent if one looked at them entirely from the performance point of view; but everything depended on whether the chief would go for results alone, because Mandy was by no means a top class event rider in the making. She would be hopeless if she was separated from the pretty bay horse.

Balthazar was a splendid horse; big, brave, scopey and capable of producing a good dressage test. And whilst Viv had been well taught and was a good rider, it was true to say that every mistake Balthazar made could be directly attributed to her inattention. Viv had everything going for her, she had the ideal horse, the ability, the opportunity, but somehow her heart wasn't in it. She didn't have the temperament or the dedication for a tough competitive sport like eventing. She resented the discipline, rules irked her, routine bored her, attention to detail made her impatient. Nevertheless, in spite of all this, Viv and Balthazar could not be discounted.

As for Alice, she was certainly dedicated, but in her own inimitable way. She was tough, and she was determined, and she had a horse of a like mind in The Talisman. One got the impression that, even if the chief decided not to chose them for the team, they would make their own way up the eventing ladder in the end. Perhaps this was a sign that he would chose them. I didn't know.

I looked along the row at their faces. Mandy looked absolutely petrified; Alice wore her see-if-I-care-anyway expression and rather a lot of green acne oitnment, and Viv's face was totally blank. Two of them will be disappointed I thought, but as it happened, I was wrong.

'In a few seconds' time, I shall read out the names of the team members for the junior trial,' the chief barked. 'There will be five names, comprising four team members and a reserve. The identity of the reserve will not be decided until just before the trial. The reason for this is that the choice of the final team may not be wholly dependent upon ability. Many things will have to be considered; emotional stability, fitness, accident.' He looked at us severely over the lecture stand as if he suspected we might not agree that this was fair.

He picked up the top sheet of paper. 'The team for the junior trial is as follows,' he announced. 'Elaine Elliot,

Phillip Hastings, Alice Merryman, Vivienne Tintoft, Amanda Willis.'

Everyone whose name had been included let out a long sigh of relief, and then, as it occurred to us whose name had been omitted, our necks swivelled towards the person sitting on the end of the row, and we all stared at Selina. Selina smiled back at us in a serene manner.

The chief marched out from behind his lecture stand. He handed a pile of memoranda to Selina. 'Be kind enough to hand these out, Miss er. . .' he said, 'and perhaps you should take this opportunity to explain yourself to your fellow students.' He favoured us with a curt nod and strode off as if he had a train to catch. The door banged shut behind him.

Selina stood up and began to hand out the memoranda giving each of us the benefit of her bright, schoolmistressy smile.

'For a start,' she informed us, 'I'm not Selina Gibbons at all. Selina was unfortunate enough to break a leg whilst out hunting with the Cottesmore and was unable to take her place. I was allowed to come instead, and my name is Jane Lejeune.' She paused expectantly, awaiting some reaction to this piece of information, but we were all too taken aback to do or say anything.

Viv recovered first. 'Wait a minute,' she said, 'you're not *that* Jane Lejeune, the one who does all sorts of different things and then writes about it in the *Sunday Times*? You're not the one who took a job as trainee sales-assistant at my old man's biggest store and wrote about all the fiddles!'

Selina inclined her head in a modest little gesture of acknowledgement. 'I'm afraid so,' she said.

Viv collapsed back in her seat. 'Blimey,' she exclaimed in an awed tone, 'it's a wonder the old man didn't have the hide off you.' She looked at Selina with a new respect.

I suppose I should have guessed, after all, I had been there when Selina had been unmasked by Mr Tintoft. I had heard it all, but then the name Jane Lejeune had meant nothing to me because I had never read the *Sunday Times*, the only newspaper the Fanes ever took was *Horse & Hound*.

'Do you mean you're not really a student?' I said, mystified. 'Do you mean you don't want to event at all?'

'Certainly not,' Selina said firmly, 'I already have a very promising career in journalism.'

Now that she had admitted it, I wondered why I hadn't suspected something like this before. There had been clues enough – the typewriter, the endless correspondence, the curiosity, the professional camera under her bed, the lengthy telephone calls.

'You're not going to write about us though, surely?' Phillip said in an incredulous voice. 'Who would be interested if you did? Wouldn't it have been better to have infiltrated the eventing world at the top?'

'Not at all, Phillip,' Selina said, with a gracious smile. 'I could hardly have held my own at the top, and the famous faces are already very well documented. But who knows about the people struggling to get a foothold on the bottom rung of the ladder? Who knows the discomfort, the sweat, the heartache, the *agony* suffered by the hidden people of eventing?' She beamed at him winningly. 'I think people are going to be *most* interested.'

I could see her point, but Mandy's mouth sagged. 'You don't mean we're going to be in the papers – not the *Sundays*,' she said aghast, 'I don't know what my dad will say when he knows.'

'Only with your permission, of course,' Selina said hastily, 'and naturally, if you would prefer, I can change your names and you would remain quite anonymous.'

'And it is the *Sunday Times*,' Phillip pointed out, 'it isn't as if it's the *News of the World*.' He seemed rather delighted with the idea.

'Well, I suppose if it isn't in the *News of the World*,' Mandy said doubtfully, 'it might be all right, because my dad might not even see it.'

Alice, who had sat silently throughout all these revelations, and now had her grounds for disliking Selina removed in one fell swoop, came to life. 'You certainly fooled me,' she said grudgingly, 'you could pass for a potential eventer any day.'

This was praise indeed from someone like Alice, and Selina preened. 'I did have a marvellous horse though,' she admitted, 'and hours of expert coaching before I came; but I was rather good, wasn't I?'

'But now you're not in the team,' Alice went on, 'what about the horse? Because if he's going spare, you could lend him to Annemarie, then at least she'd have something to ride for the rest of the course.'

It seemed a splendid idea. 'But I'm afraid it can't be done,' Selina said with regret, 'the horse I rode isn't Flame Thrower at all, he's an intermediate event horse and he belongs to Hans Gelderhol. He's being collected tomorrow to go back into training for Burghley.'

'So it *was* the horse I remembered,' I exclaimed, 'and I had assumed he might just be related!' Altogether, I seemed to have been rather dim-witted about the whole affair.

'I must admit to feeling a qualm when I discovered that you had trained with Hans Gelderhol,' Selina admitted, 'especially when you mentioned the similarity to the horse he had been eventing at the time.'

'No wonder you were so good,' Alice said, with a smart return to her previous acerbic form, 'riding an intermediate event horse.'

Selina chose to ignore this remark. 'Well, now that there is absolutely no need for secrecy,' she said in a satisfied tone, 'I shall spend the rest of the weekend taking photographs.' She beamed round at us, tore the chief's latest memorandum into tiny pieces, tossed them into the air in a gesture of smug finality, and left the lecture hall before the pieces had even reached the ground.

We, who were left, looked at one another, dumbfounded.

'Wouldn't you just believe it,' Alice trumpeted, 'the *Sunday Times*!'

114

Later that day I rang Nick at the kennels to give him the good news. 'That's fantastic,' he said, 'not that I had any doubts anyway, I knew you'd do it.'

'Would you do something for me?' I asked him. 'Would you call in and see the Fanes before you take the hound draft and tell them for me?' I wanted them to know, but I wasn't at all anxious to speak to Henrietta or Nigella again, not until after the trial. I had enough to occupy my mind as it was.

'I was going to tell you about the Fanes,' he said, 'I don't know if you've heard from them recently, but I dropped by the other day and it seems that wonder woman's left.'

'I know,' I said, 'they came to tell me.'

'So you probably already know,' he said, 'that they're selling up.'

I didn't believe it. 'They can't be,' I said, 'I knew they had problems, but the bank has given them a fortnight to put things right – I know it's true because Lady Jennifer told me herself.' But even as I said it my elation started to ebb away and a familiar sinking feeling began in my chest.

'I don't know about that,' Nick said, 'but there's a *For Sale* notice at the bottom of the drive, and when I arrived the girls were loading pictures into the shooting brake.'

I remembered the dusty, darkened oil paintings lining the staircase and the galleried landings. The best had long since been taken away, leaving bare, oblong patches on the walls. I knew the ones that were left were hardly worth selling; they were just rather poor portraits of Fane ancestors painted by unknown artists. Everything of value had already gone from Havers Hall; Henrietta had sold her Vile secretaire in order to pay for Legend, and I myself had carried a valuable Cantonese vase up the escalators to Harrods Fine Art department so that we could pay off the saddler, the corn merchant, the blacksmith . . .

'Nick,' I said, 'they *can't* have decided already, they *can't* have given up hope, not just like that.'

'I think they must have decided,' he said, 'they've already told us to . . .' he tailed off, not wanting to continue.

There was a silence.

'Oh no,' I whispered, 'they haven't . . . they couldn't . . . Oh, Nick, not the *horses*.'

'No,' he admitted, 'not yet, they're not – they're a bit . . .'

I knew what he was trying to say; that after a hard season's hunting they were all too thin. A few months out at grass at this time of year would make all the difference, especially now there was no need to shut off half the park for the winter.

'Elaine . . . are you still there?'

'Yes,' I said, 'I'm still here.'

'They told me – Henrietta told me, that they asked you to give up Legend.'

'They did, and I almost considered it, but Lady Jennifer wrote to me, she said that I shouldn't.' In her letter, I thought, she had made light of their difficulties, she had said it was only a temporary setback, and they had a fortnight's grace and were optimistic that something would turn up. She had probably told me this knowing all the time that nothing would turn up, having already instructed the Estate Agents to call. Such an action was typical of someone who devoted her life to the welfare of others, without giving a thought to her own perilous circumstances.

'I'm glad you *didn't* consider it,' Nick said in a grim voice, 'whatever their problems are, you must *never* consider giving up Legend, he's your future.'

'But what about *their* future?' I asked him miserably. 'The horses haven't any future at all, and I don't think I shall be able to bear it.'

'Would you be able to bear it any better if they were sold at auction?' he wanted to know. 'Would you have preferred the Fanes to do that? Because I'm surprised they *didn't*. They would have got meat money for them, after all; so that must be something to be thankful for.'

I tried to feel thankful. I knew that being humanely destroyed in their own familiar fields was far preferable to being sold on the open market; to being loaded on to one of the hellships which transported meat cattle on the hoof to the continent, then being docked and herded into huge container lorries and driven for days without food or water, to be finally butchered in some foreign abattoir. I knew I would have sold Legend, I would have sold my soul, I would have died before I could let that happen. Yes, I knew it was better, but I couldn't feel thankful, it was too unbearably, heartbreakingly sad for that.

'I thought we might have been able to find homes for them,' I said, 'I thought there might be some way . . .'

'Look, Elaine,' Nick said, 'I'm beginning to think I shouldn't have told you.'

'If you hadn't,' I told him, 'I would never have forgiven you.'

'But as I have told you, you must make me a promise.'

I knew what that would be. After all, I had already promised Lady Jennifer the same thing.

'You mustn't think about it, worry about it, until after the junior trial,' he said, 'the house won't sell, just like that. It'll take months, perhaps years to find a buyer. And the horses are safe for two months at least. Nothing's going to happen yet, *nothing*,' he emphasized, 'is going to change before the junior trial. Promise me Elaine, that you won't try to do *anything*, that you won't let it spoil your chances next week – *promise*.'

'I promise,' I said. After all, what else could I say.

'And after the trial,' he said, 'we'll worry about it then; we'll talk about it, and if there's a way, if there's anything at all we can do, we'll do it.'

'All right,' I agreed.

'But we won't part with Legend,' he assured me, 'whatever we may decide, it won't be that.'

'Thank you,' I said, and miserable though I was, I was grateful and gladdened that he cared enough about the Fanes even to want to discuss their problems, when not so very long ago, he had despised them.

'By the way,' Nick said, 'did you get any replies to your advertisement?'

'The chief replied,' I told him, 'he offered me a job. I can stay here and work on the yards as a member of the junior staff.'

'And will you stay?' he asked.

'It looks as if there won't be any alternative,' I said.

14

No Substitute

I woke because someone was shaking me. I sat up in bed feeling alarmed. I knew it couldn't be Selina because stertorous breathing was coming from the other bed. After an energetic afternoon with her camera, she was dead to the world.

'Elaine!' Viv's voice hissed urgently. 'Bloody hell, I thought you'd never wake up!'

'Viv,' I whispered anxiously, 'what's wrong? Are you ill or something?' In the moonlight filtering through the Duke of Newcastle's ineffective curtains, I could now make out the shape of her, kneeling beside my bed.

'I've come to say goodbye,' she said in a low voice. 'I've decided to take off. Now. Tonight.'

'Take off?' I struggled up into a sitting position, hardly able to take it in because I was still half asleep. 'What on earth do you mean? You *can't* be leaving, not *now*. Not in the middle of the *night*!'

'Sssssh,' Viv hissed urgently, 'don't go and wake *her*,' she nodded towards the dark hump in the next bed, 'she's all I need!'

'But why are you going?' I still couldn't believe it. 'What about Balthazar – are you taking him?' For one minute I could see her, muffling his hoofs with the Duke of Newcastle's threadbare towels, in order to lead him silently out of the yards.

'No, I'm leaving him,' Viv said, 'for Annemarie.'

'For *Annemarie*?' I stared at her, stupified.

'Look Elaine,' she said, 'I would have gone before, I'm not really into all this eventing, you know I'm not. I just sort of slipped into it, and after what happened to Annemarie's horse – well, I know it isn't for me, but I wanted to hang on to be sure I'd got a place in the team, and now I know I have, I can leave. It's as simple as that.'

'You'd leave Balthazar for *Annemarie*,' I said, appalled, 'after what she did to her own horse?'

'That was partly my fault anyway,' Viv said, 'and Balthazar's more the horse for someone as ambitious as Annemarie than ever that poor little bay was. She'll find a different problem when she rides Balthazar, and it won't be pushing him to the limits of his capabilities, it'll be letting him go as much as he wants to. I've no worries about him, he can look after himself.'

I could see that this might be true; '*I* wouldn't do it,' I told her, 'I wouldn't let anyone else ride Legend.'

'But then,' Viv said, 'not everyone's as selfish as you are.'

There wasn't time to feel offended. 'Where will you go?' I asked her. 'Will you go back to your gran?'

'Well I shan't go back to the old man,' she said bitterly. 'He really had plans for me, I can tell you. Six months with this top eventing coach, six months there, a string of event horses – I'd probably even have ended up at the Reitschule. No, I've had enough of eventing, thanks Elaine, you're welcome to it.'

Although I knew in my heart that she was right to leave, I didn't want her to go now, not alone, in the middle of the night. It was dangerous. Anything could happen to an unaccompanied young girl. 'You're not to go now,' I said, grabbing her arm, 'wait until the morning, wait until daylight. I'm not going to let you go. I'm going to wake the others.'

'Elaine,' said Viv in a voice of deadly earnestness, 'if you even so much as open your mouth, I'll knock you out cold with the lamp.'

'*Viv*!' I was aghast, moreso because I knew she meant it.

'There's nothing you can do to stop me,' she said, 'I've made up my mind, and if I'd realized you were going to be so awkward about it, I wouldn't have bothered waking you.'

'Oh, *Viv*,' I said sadly, 'what will you do now?'

'Well,' she said, considering it, 'to tell the truth I've always thought I might like to have a go at acting, you

120

know. I might audition for RADA or LAMDA, or some-where like that; it's hard to get in, I know, but I might just make it, and that's something Mr Fixit really *can't* interfere with.'

But he'll try, I thought, he'll really try. She got up and made her way silently to the door.

'Viv,' I said, 'he only interferes because he loves you.'

She paused. 'Yes,' she said shortly, 'maybe.'

'And I'm sorry you're leaving,' I said, 'I'm really sorry.'

'So am I,' she whispered as she slipped out of the door. 'If I'd known I wasn't staying, I wouldn't have cut my nails.'

I lay back on my lumpy pillow and I heard the Duke of Newcastle's back door click shut behind her. I lay awake for a long time thinking of the slight girl with the orange hair driving along the dark, empty roads, and the man with the silk tie and the pale green Rolls Royce who, although he knew many things, had never learned that money, ambition, or even love, were no substitute for freedom, understanding and respect.

'Step into the office for a moment, Miss Elliott,' said the chief as he marched along the walkway in front of the stable where I was strapping Legend.

I replaced Legend's rug and roller and hurried after him, dropping my grooming kit box outside the stable door and kicking over the bottom latch.

The chief took up his position behind his desk and ledged his beautiful boots, out of habit toes up heels down, on the brass footrail. He took off his tweed cap and laid it on top of a pile of memoranda.

'Have you any money?' he asked.

I stared at him in astonishment. 'Not very much,' I admitted, 'about forty pounds.'

'Any savings? Any private income?'

'No,' I said, 'nothing at all.'

'What about your father,' he demanded, 'is he rich?'

'No,' I said, 'I'm afraid not.' I was beginning to feel rather alarmed.

'You do realize,' said the chief, 'that eventing is a very expensive sport?'

'Oh yes,' I assured him, 'I do.'

'And that most people, if they don't happen to have well-heeled connections, need a sponsor in order to meet their expenses.'

'Yes,' I said. I couldn't see for the life of me what he was getting at.

'Then how are you, Miss Elliot, on your fifty pounds a week, less stoppages, going to afford it?'

'Well,' I said carefully, 'my horse won't cost me anything to keep . . .'

'You'll have to keep him shod,' the chief pointed out, 'you have to provide his equipment, clothing for yourself, registration fees, entry fees, petrol, veterinary fees. Even leg washes and worming powders,' he said, 'cost money.'

I couldn't think of a reply to any of this.

'Have you ever heard of the Horse Trials Support Group?' he asked.

I said I thought I had, but then again, I couldn't be sure.

'It comes under the umbrella of the BHS,' he said, 'and every so often, when funds allow them to do so, they offer their support to potential top class event riders with promising horses in order that they may continue to event – usually riders with a good deal of winning form and experience behind them.'

I wondered what he was going to suggest. I hadn't a good deal of winning form and experience behind me.

'I have already had a preliminary talk with the chairman,' said the chief, 'and I put forward a suggestion that they might consider giving you some assistance in the form of a modest grant.'

'A grant? For me? To help with Legend?' It seemed hardly possible.

'Of course,' he said, 'it is by no means certain that they will agree . . .'

I still couldn't grasp it. 'Do you mean they would give me *money*?'

'Miss Elliot,' the chief said in a testy voice, 'a grant usually consists of money, and in the case of a grant from the Horse Trials Support Group, it is usually a contribution, a percentage of travelling and competition expenses.'

'But they'll never give money to *me*,' I said, 'they've never even heard of *me*.'

'That may well be true,' he agreed, 'nevertheless, they are going to brief a member of the selection board for the Junior Olympics who will be officiating at the junior trial, and as a result of his report, they may decide that you are worthy of consideration, and you may be allowed to put your case before a special committee.'

I stared at him in amazement, and already my mind was churning with possibilities; alarming, incredible possibilities.

'I *will*?'

'You might,' the chief replied in a dry tone, 'if you perform well at the junior trial.'

I reeled out of the office, hardly daring to contemplate the viability of the plan already forming in my mind. If the grant from the Horse Trials Support Group was big enough, it might be utilized to bail the Fanes out of their present difficulty.

'Gordon Bennett,' Alice commented morosely, as with an appalling succession of crashing blows, Annemarie and Balthazar demolished the triple combination, leaving the coloured poles scattered around the jumping arena as if they were no more than matchsticks. 'She'll have to be put in reserve. If we have to have her in the team, we'll be sunk.'

Viv's abrupt removal from the scholarship course had caused something of a furore the following morning, when the letter she had pushed under the office door for the attention of the chief had been discovered. Mr Tintoft had been summoned, and he had arrived without delay, spending almost an hour with the chief, but at the end of it, Balthazar had been formally offered to Annemarie, and the chief had announced that Miss Tintoft had resigned from the course for 'family reasons'.

Now though, we were left with the problem of putting

together Annemarie and Balthazar with less than a week to go before the junior trial.

Due to her high-powered instruction in Germany, Annemarie was an excellent, correct, disciplined rider, but compared to the average English rider, she appeared to be rather stiff, unyielding, and unsympathetic. She had schooled her own part-bred Hanoverian horse herself, and he was accustomed to her style of riding, but Balthazar, being a much longer-striding, free-moving horse, used to Viv's more relaxed approach, was not, and he resented it.

There had been difficulties aplenty over the cross-country course, but now, in the confines of the show-jumping arena, it seemed to be even worse. The chief had devoted most of his time to trying to overcome their problems; but as there was not enough time to reschool the horse to respond to Annemarie's expectations, it had to be the other way round; Annemarie had to adapt herself to Balthazar. She was trying very hard, but it was not easy for either of them.

We, who were the rest of the team for the junior trial, sat on our horses and watched from outside the arena, biting our glove ends as Balthazar fought against Annemarie on his approach to the fences, throwing up his head, hollowing his back, and dropping his hind legs on to the poles. Timber scattered, wings rocked, the powerful hooves flew, as Annemarie over-collected the chestnut horse, chopping his flowing stride, upsetting his natural balance and bungling his take-offs. The chief held his hands over his ears as the sound of falling timber went on all around him, and yelled at her to relax, to give more rein, to try somehow, anyhow, to achieve some rapport with the big, confused gelding. To give Annemarie her due, she improved a little at every session, and she never uttered one word of complaint, but in the short time left to us it became clear that Alice was right. If we had to call on Annemarie and Balthazar for the team, our chances of success would be virtually non-existent.

A few days before the junior trial, the chief staged a mock trial of his own. We rode the dressage test we were to ride on the day, we went round the show-jumps, and we finished by riding the whole of the cross-country course. The results were hardly encouraging.

Somehow we all managed to produce abysmal dressage tests; even Phillip, who was never less than consistent, got a poor mark. Legend blew up completely, shied at the markers he had seen every day for the past three weeks, refused to settle, and got the worst mark of all. Mandy lost her way three times, blundering along hopelessly, until the chief was forced to intervene with directions. The Talisman refused to walk and did all the walking movements at a jog trot, and the best score was achieved by Annemarie and Balthazar which, while it gave a much-needed boost to their morale, was pretty depressing for everyone else.

We scraped round the show-jumps, with two clears; Phillip and Mandy. Legend took a pole off the double, The Talisman managed to knock the brush fence over, which is practically impossible to do, and Annemarie and Balthazar knocked down every other fence.

Things were hardly any better when it came to the cross-country. Legend was still far too exuberant, despite the fact that I had doubled his riding-in time, and got into trouble almost immediately at the uphill double, pulling away from me at the approach and landing too far in, screwing himself up and over the second part by a miracle, but losing me over his shoulder in the process. I was unhurt, but over-cautious after that, and we finished with three penalties.

Phillip, who seemed to be jinxed, fell into the lake when the amazing roan lost its footing unexpectedly on the approach to the telegraph pole and vanished in a cloud of spray, reappearing on the other side of the obstacle trotting energetically towards the bank, with Phillip floundering after him. This made for a nightmare round as far as Phillip was concerned – sopping wet clothes, slippery reins, a saddle like a waterchute and, to cap it all, a severe attack of stomach cramp, which the chief supposed to be brought on by nerves.

Mandy and Fox Me flew round in their customary charmed manner, but due to lack of brainpower missed out two fences entirely which meant instant elimination from the cross-country phase. Finally, Alice suffered a crashing fall off The Talisman when he unexpectedly applied his brakes at the zig-zag rails. She galloped through the finish with her face awash with blood – it turned out to be only a nosebleed, but it was very nerve-racking all the same. The round accomplished by Annemarie and Balthazar was a battle from start to finish and appallingly slow, but at least they didn't hit a single fence which was an improvement on previous rounds.

After this disastrous showing, we rode back to the yard feeling stunned. The chief, surprisingly, didn't appear to be unduly concerned, and when we returned to the Duke of Newcastle, after attending to our horses, we found that Selina, who had had a field day with her camera during the mock trial, and whose suitcases were already packed against her removal the next morning, had cooked a farewell celebratory supper.

It was at the precise moment that she was walking into the room bearing aloft a cracked casserole dish, preceded by a delicious aroma of casseroled chicken with herbs, cream, and white wine, that Phillip, who had been spasmodically bowed over by his stomach cramp, suddenly slumped on to the table, and fell sideways, and in slow-motion, into a senseless heap on the linoleum.

Less than an hour later he was wheeled into the operating theatre to have his appendix removed.

15
Junior Trials

'Gordon Bennett,' Alice remarked, staring down into a chasm the width and length of which would have accommodated a family saloon car, situated below some hefty timber rails. 'I don't know why they didn't go the whole hog and line it with broken bottles.' I knew how she felt. It was a tough cross-country course for the junior trial.

We had marched around it with the chief the previous evening, and now, in the early morning before we began to prepare for the dressage, we walked round it more slowly on our own. Two miles of varied terrain and eighteen difficult fences under a sky which, if gathering clouds were anything to go by, promised the added complication of rain. I had never doubted Legend's ability to tackle any course so far, but now I thought of the obstacles I had seen, the table, the blind drop, the Normandy Bank, the coffin, the birch rails set on the edge of a fast-running stream with a watery landing, and the gaping trakehner, and I trembled.

Annemarie stared at the fences with her lips pressed into a tight line. If she was frightened, she wasn't going to admit it. Mandy was pale, but then she was always pale, and as there was nothing left of her nails to bite, and her hair was enclosed in a hairnet at all times on the instructions of the chief, she gnawed her knuckles instead. Only Alice showed no outward sign of nervousness and, as a concession to appearances at the trial, she had purchased some spotcover makeup. Unfortunately it was a pasty pink, and the combination of the makeup, the angry eruption of the spots, her own sallow skin, and her mustard yellow team sweatshirt was pretty dire.

The team sweatshirts were a not altogether welcome surprise because they were casual dress uniform for the trial and turned us into walking advertisements for our sponsor. Across our chests we carried the slogan HISSEY'S PICKLES LEAD

THE FIELD, and below it a pickled onion and a gherkin wore jolly smiles and silly little riding hats. The general effect was distressing, but as they had been presented to us with great ceremony by Felix Hissey himself, we could hardly refuse to wear them. Only Alice gloried in hers, mainly to annoy the chief who winced every time he saw us wearing them.

We walked on, pacing our distances, checking landings and take-offs for the going, working out the shortest route between the fences, deciding which line to take over fences which offered alternatives, wading into the stream to test the bed for stones, holes and firmness, calculating speeds, strides, and the effect of uphill and downhill gradients. None of us had very much to say. How different it would have been, I thought wistfully, if it had been Viv, Selina and Phillip in the team; then it would have been almost enjoyable – and more important, then we would have had a chance.

The dressage was scheduled to begin at nine, and my courage suffered another setback when I discovered that I had been drawn first. After all that had gone before, the horrendous mock trial, and Phillip's appendicitis, it seemed the final straw. 'Oh well,' I told Legend, as we set out at a quarter to eight under a sky of unrelenting grey cloud, 'somebody had to be first, and at least it will soon be over and done with.'

Under the chief's critical eye, we had all schooled our horses thoroughly and diligently the previous day, and as soon as I put Legend to work I could feel that it had paid off. He was no longer bursting out of his skin, he was alert, responsive and sensible.

At eight thirty I rode back to the temporary stabling to change. I stripped off the Hissey sweatshirt and the jeans I had worn to protect my breeches, tied my stock, buffed up my boots, put on my good navy coat and brushed my hat. The rest of the team, supervised by the chief, unfamiliar in a suit and a bowler hat, busied themselves with Legend, oiling his hooves, brushing out his tail, wiping the bits of the double bridle which had been purchased by means of the

Fanes' training fund. Just before mounting I skimmed through the printed test for the last time to refresh my memory.

With less than fifteen minutes to go, more riders were now working their horses steadily in the exercising area. Knots of people could be seen gathering outside the little grandstand at one end of the dressage arena, and the judges were strolling across the grass towards their caravan. Amongst them, I knew, were the selectors for the Junior Olympics, and one of them had a special interest in me. We may not have a chance as a team, I thought, but I must do well, I *must*, for everyone's sake.

I worked Legend gently behind the arena, waiting for the starting steward to give me the signal which would allow us a few valuable minutes inside the boards before the test began. I could think of nothing but the importance of performing a good test in front of the people inside the judges' caravan. Nothing else mattered. I knew that Legend had never been on such top form – the month of instruction and fitness training had made an enormous difference to us both, and if we couldn't do it today, we probably never would.

The signal came, we trotted forward into the arena, and as we did so the clouds suddenly parted and everywhere was bathed in sunshine. The white boards sparkled, the black letters danced, and shimmering auburn highlights appeared on Legend's silken neck.

We stood at the scoreboards, holding our breath as the scorer mounted the ladder. My score went up first. It was sixty-four. It seemed to be a good score, but everything now depended on the general standard. The next score went up. Seventy. Then the next, sixty-eight. And the next. One hundred and five. Yes, it was a good one and I felt myself sag at the knees with relief. Alice's was the next score and it was quite a way down the board. When she had seen her drawn number she had not been too dismayed because she was not at all superstitious, but, 'Wouldn't you just believe it,' she had commented in an acid voice, '*thirteen*.' The score which appeared opposite her name was a respectable seventy-one.

Annemarie, who had produced a surprisingly fluent test, marred only by Balthazar's occasional shows of irritated head-shaking and tail-swishing, was given sixty-nine, and Mandy, whose test had been threatened by one black moment when she had hesitated, unsure of the next movement when circling back on to the track at sitting trot, and had been saved by Fox Me who slipped into a canter as they hit the letter, thus anticipating at a most fortuitous moment and reminding her of what came next, was given a seventy-nine. By the end of the score posting, I was fourth individual overall, and the Hissey Training Scholarship Team were lying third out of nine teams.

It was an unbelievably marvellous beginning, and it had an instant effect on our damaged morale. Alice let out a mighty whoop of joy, Mandy continued to stare up at the boards as if she had seen a heavenly vision, and Annemarie smiled for the first time in two weeks. As for me, I stopped thinking of myself as an individual, and remembered that we were supposed to be a team; we *were* a team – and it was high time that we began to think, act, and ride like a team. A chance to ride for the scholarship team in the junior trial had been the one thing that all of us had wanted. Well, we were here, we were lying third after the first phase, and now we would go out there and fight.

'We can do it,' I told the others, 'I'm *sure* we can do it.'

'Not before I have taken my photograph, if you wouldn't mind!' Selina, sportingly clad in a quilted anorak and culottes, was already engaged in journalistic operations, removing anxious competitors and their supporters from her path in her most charmingly authoritative manner. 'I'm really *so* sorry – Would you excuse me? Will you move a little to the right, Mandy? Could you look up at the scoreboards for me? Would it be possible for you to look a little more worried, Elaine? – Oh my goodness,' she said in a pained voice, 'where did you get those *terrible* jerseys?'

130

Mandy jumped first in phase two, the show-jumping. It was not a difficult course; we confidently expected Fox Me to go clear and we were not disappointed. They cantered round in a blithe manner, making nothing of the course, clearing the spreads, the combinations, and the uprights, and trotted out to a scattering of applause.

Alice was next and as the bell rang she pushed The Talisman into a canter and they went through the start towards the first jump. There was no doubt that Alice had benefitted enormously from her month with the chief. Her seat was much stronger and she was far more positive and co-ordinated in her riding. I watched with a thumping heart as she jumped a clear round knocking, but not dislodging, the gate and the wall. Now it was Annemarie, and this really would be the test.

Balthazar bounded through the start and Annemarie, in her anxiety not to over-collect him, let him go too fast in the first fence and his hind legs trailed through the brush. Luckily, this was unpenalized but it was not a promising start. They jumped the next two fences clear and approached the double. I held my breath as Balthazar sailed over the first part, took two flying strides, and leapt out without any trouble at all. Now there was a wall for which Annemarie sat down and shortened him, too much I thought, far too much, but no, they were over, and already lengthening towards the water, clearing it, and on into the triple combination, over the first part, two perfectly timed strides, over the second part, three strides, and over the last. It was an incredible performance for Annemarie and Balthazar and Annemarie obviously thought so as well because she seemed to lose her concentration with the relief of it. Balthazar picked up too much speed, and galloped, hopelessly fast, into an upright plank jump, Annemarie caught him back in the nick of time, Balthazar climbed over it, and by a miracle managed not to dislodge the top plank, but by then, their luck had run out and they took the last fence in a shower of poles, scattering a row of conifers, breaking two pot plants, and even knocking over one of the wings. Nevertheless, we were all delighted, because for Balthazar and Annemarie, a round with only four faults was a great achievement.

Having stayed at the ringside to watch Annemarie's round, I now ran for Legend, took him twice over the practice fence, and rode into the ring and through the start, feeling nervous, but optimistic. Legend jumped a perfect round, flowing over the fences, never putting a polished hoof out of place, and we cantered back to our swelling band of supporters, triumphant.

The Hissey Training Scholarship Team had now gathered quite a following; Viv had arrived; so had Alice's mother, who was an older, gruffer, taller version of Alice; Mandy's parents were there, filled with awe and excitement but rather clueless about what was going on; even some relations of Annemarie had come from Halesowen in lieu of her parents who were still in Germany. There was Selina with her camera; there was even Felix Hissey himself, rotund, beaming with delight at our unexpectedly good showing so far, and of course, there was the chief, who, when he received the news that after the show-jumping the team had moved up to second place, and I was lying third individual overall, gave a curtly satisfied nod, as if it was no more than he would have expected anyway.

But it was now the end of the first day, and nobody had arrived for me; not the Fanes, not my father, not even Nick. I couldn't imagine why this should be and I felt hurt and offended. I knew the Fanes had problems of their own to contend with, but they had all promised, even Lady Jennifer had promised in her letter, that they would attend.

'Never mind,' I told Legend as we walked together across the sunlit turf towards the temporary stabling, 'they'll come tomorrow. I know they'll come tomorrow.' They had better come tomorrow, I thought angrily, after all I am planning to do for them.

The next morning I stood outside Legend's temporary stable wearing Nigella's lucky red and blue jumper, the side seams of which I had cobbled together to give it some semblance of shape. I'm wearing the Fanes' colours, I thought, and they will never know. I had no idea what had happened to them, to my father, and to Nick, but I had given up all hope of seeing them now, and I had no room in my mind for speculation. Every scrap of concentration was directed towards riding clear across country, for the team, for the selection committee, for the Horse Trials Support Group Grant, for the chief, for Felix Hissey, and for Legend. I slipped on my number cloth, put on my hat, fastened my safety harness and called good luck to Alice and The Talisman as they set out towards the start with the chief walking beside them.

Mandy had already ridden her cross-country, and Fox Me had gone brilliantly, cantering through the finish with one refusal at the blind drop, and no time penalties. He stood now, spent, as Mandy sluiced him with buckets of warmed water, his nose almost touching the ground, water cascading off his belly and his chin.

Annemarie, second of the Hissey Team to ride, limped in leading Balthazar. She had sustained a bruised thigh and a thorough soaking when the big chestnut had fallen on top of her at the running stream, and she had a gathering bruise on her cheekbone where she had fallen again at the angled triple. Despite this, she was triumphant, and Balthazar, though showing vermilion on the insides of his distended nostrils and pouring with sweat, looked magnificent, and hadn't a scratch. 'He's a fantastic, wonderful horse,' Annemarie declared, 'another month and I shall have his measure.' This was a new, humbled Annemarie to the one we had first known, and Viv, collecting buckets and scrapers for the washdown, caught my eye and winked.

The next horse returned to the stable block horribly lame and bleeding from a deep gash above his hock. I turned away and closed my heart to it. After Annemarie's accident, I had confessed my doubts about the moral aspect of testing a horse to its limits to the chief. He had answered my questions by replying that there was no clearcut answer, but that all event riders asked themselves the same question sooner or later and could only answer for themselves and with their own conscience. I had made a bargain with myself which was that if I ever felt that Legend had stopped enjoying it, if I ever had cause to suspect his soundness, fitness, or mental attitude, I would stop.

Putting these thoughts and my worries about the absence of the Fanes, my father and Nick firmly out of my mind, I led Legend out of his stable, tightened his girth and surcingle, checked his bandages, boots and bridle, smeared his legs with vaseline from the communal tub, secured the headpiece of his bridle to his forelock plait with tape to minimise the risk of losing the bridle in the event of a fall, and mounted up. I left the yard to a chorus of heartfelt good wishes. Both Alice and I had to go clear if the Hissey team were to hold their position in second place.

I rode towards the chief who was waiting for me in the exercising area where the riders who were to go before me were warming up. 'The Talisman is over fence one and two,' said the commentator. I trotted up to the chief feeling my throat tighten. Legend flexed his neck and threw out his toes as if he was in a show class, his black plaits sharp and firm against his bay neck.

'The Talisman is clear at number four . . .'

The chief made a wry face and held up crossed fingers.

I worked Legend steadily, gave him his pipe-opener, and resumed some slow, sober work at the trot and canter. I could feel his eager excitement and his impatience but he didn't lose his manners.

'The Talisman is clear at number eight and nine . . .'

I cantered Legend in some slow figures of eight, doing some deep breathing to calm my nerves.

'The Talisman is clear at fourteen and fifteen . . .'

'Good old Alice,' I thought, 'whatever else she might be, she's a trooper.'

'The Talisman is clear at sixteen and seventeen . . .' and then a ghastly silence until, blessedly, 'The Talisman is clear at the final fence. No time penalties.'

Now it was up to me.

The chief walked me down to the start. Beyond the finish I could see the saddle being dragged off The Talisman as Alice went to weigh-in. Selina was taking photographs.

As the starter began the countdown, Legend stood like a rock. I could almost hear his heart beating.

'Eighteen, seventeen, sixteen . . .'

'*Elaine*!'

'. . . fifteen, fourteen, thirteen . . .'

'ELAINE!'

I tried to ignore it, but I couldn't. I turned.

'I thought we'd be too late,' Henrietta panted.

'. . . twelve, eleven, ten . . .'

'Go away,' I implored her, thinking that whatever frightful news she was bringing, I couldn't possibly hear it now. 'I'm busy – this is *important*.'

'. . . nine, eight, seven . . .'

'But so is this important,' Henrietta said in a desperate voice.

'Not *that* important, Miss Fane,' said the chief firmly. He took Henrietta by the collar of her anorak and tried to pull her away backwards, out of range.

'Don't,' Henrietta shouted, struggling red-faced, 'I only want . . .'

'. . . six, five, four . . .' The starter struggled to hang on to his concentration.

'. . . to tell Elaine that we're RICH!' Henrietta squealed.

'. . . three, two, one – GO!'

Legend shot like a bullet past the starter, covering the turf in mighty leaps. I knew I shouldn't be thinking of anything except the course, the team, and the selection committee, but I just had to know. I looked back.

'What do you mean?' I shouted, and I saw that Henrietta had managed to wriggle out of her anorak and was now flying after Legend in her purple tights and legwarmers, and that after her came the starter, and after him the chief, still gripping the anorak.

'The picture in your bedroom – the Elizabethan lady,' Henrietta shrieked, 'it's worth a FORTUNE!' At this point, unable to sustain such a headlong flight in her stiletto-heeled shoes, she fell face-down on the grass and was

135

captured by the starter, and I, feeling Legend already beginning to lengthen into the first fence, burst out laughing as he soared up and cleared it.

'It can't be true,' I told him, 'it *can't* be.'

Legend, instead of answering, rose in a beautifully effortless arc over the gaping trakehner and landed without a falter in his stride.

'Oh *Elaine*,' Lady Jennifer's voice said admiringly, 'that was *terribly* good.'

I glanced towards the direction of the voice and caught a glimpse of Lady Jennifer and my father, standing arm-in-arm. Has the whole world gone mad, I asked myself, or am I hallucinating?

Down we went towards the coffin, over the first pole, took one downhill stride, then the ditch was below us, and with one mighty uphill bound, we were over the other pole and climbing the rise towards the blind drop.

'Another Legend clear at fences two and three . . .'

The blind drop had caused a lot of trouble and it had been where Fox Me stopped, so I was ready for Legend when he faltered, not at all keen to jump into the darkness of a copse when he couldn't see anything beyond. I collected him firmly and pushed him on. He cocked his ears at it, lengthened, rose up and plummeted, throwing out his forelegs and pecking slightly on the landing. I lost a stirrup but we were over and cantering on towards the log pile. Next came the birch rails with the watery landing, and the table which, although it had looked almost unjumpable from the ground, looked perfectly feasible from the back of a horse. Legend made nothing of it.

'Another Legend clear at fences six and seven . . .'

Now we were faced with the Telegraph 'W', and as we approached it, it seemed to be a mass of jumbled angles. I knew Legend wouldn't make any sense of it until it was too late, and I had already decided to take him over the two points. I collected him, he jumped, took one short stride, and bounced over the second point. Scattered applause came from people standing at one side and the judge raised her flag.

'Another Legend clear at fence eight. . .'

Obstacle after obstacle vanished under Legend's soaring hooves and the nearer to the finish we got, the more our joint confidence increased and the easier each fence became. My heart grew lighter with every jump as I realized that we were probably going to win, that the team would retain their second place, that I wouldn't have to part with Legend, that the Fanes were going to be all right and their horses would be saved.

Finally, standing by the last fence, I saw Nick, holding in his arms the biggest bottle of champagne I had ever seen in my life.

'Another Legend clear at the last fence. No time penalties,' announced the commentator.

I almost fell out of the saddle. Somebody undid the girth and put it into my hands. Someone else threw a rug over Legend. I weighed-in in a daze. The Fanes seemed to be everywhere.

'Sothebys say it might fetch half a million,' Henrietta said in a satisfied voice as if our conversation at the countdown had not been interrupted. 'So we don't have to sell after all and we can keep the horses.'

'And we thought we'd do hunting breaks in the winter, and riding courses in the summer,' Nigella said, 'residential, of course.'

'So you need your BHSI,' Henrietta said, 'but it shouldn't be too difficult. After all, you've got your Horsemaster's, and that's a start.'

'We'll do up the house,' Nigella said. 'Every room will have hot and cold running water.'

'And we won't want to sell Legend, if that's what you're worried about,' Henrietta said. 'In fact, now that we're rich, we'll give you our share, at least,' she added, her natural caution getting the better of her, 'we'll think about it.'

'And as our home is going to be your home anyway,' Nigella said, 'you'll want to come back, won't you? Now that Mummy and your father are going to be married.'

'*Married*!'

'Oh Elaine,' Lady Jennifer trilled, her face radiant. 'Don't you think it's a *frightfully* splendid idea?'

'The gardens are very run down,' said my father confidingly, 'but I feel the terrace would make a splendid patio.'

'Excuse my butting in on what I feel sure is a private celebration,' Selina said in her most charming voice, 'but could I *possibly* trouble you for a photograph? Would you take off your hat, Elaine? And could you, Nick, just pretend to pour some champagne into it?'

The bang, as Nick opened the jeroboam, almost made Legend jump out of his skin.

'What a terribly amusing idea,' Lady Jennifer shrilled as champagne foamed and flowed into my best cross-country hat for the benefit of the *Sunday Times*.

Felix Hissey appeared at my elbow, his jolly face alight with the glory of having his team finish second and one of their number first overall and now a certainty for the Junior Olympics. There was to be a party, he announced, for everyone, but first I was to be taken to be personally congratulated by the head of the Olympic Selection Committee.

'Now?' I said, alarmed by the thought of it. 'But I can't, I have to look after Legend.' Legend, who had cantered through the finish looking fit for another twenty miles, was wearing his sweat rug and a headcollar and showing enormous interest in a packet of polo mints being opened by Nigella.

Henrietta took his rein. 'We'll look after him,' she said, 'I'll wash, and Nigella can scrape.'

'And I'll cut off his bandages and plaster him with kaolin,' said Nick. He passed the jeroboam to my father and took the saddle out of my arms. 'Go on,' he said, 'and prepare yourself for a surprise.'

I followed Felix Hissey to the judges' caravan overlooking the deserted dressage arena. He opened the door, indicated that I should precede him in a courtly manner, and shut the door smartly as soon as I mounted the steps. The head of the Selection Committee sat at the table in front of the wide window and he looked at me for a long time without speaking.

I didn't speak either. I couldn't. I had trained in his yard, I had taken his every word as gospel, I had admired him above all others; I had watched him endlessly, adoringly, as he schooled, trained, gave his attention to more talented, more attractive people than I; and yes, I had been in love with him, as young girls often are with their mentors, and I had resented the fact that to him, I was just another working pupil, just another acolyte in his firmament, and because of this I had refused his help and I had sworn that I would make it on my own. And glory, I thought suddenly, by the skin of my teeth, and by the width of my fingernails, I have got this far without him, and now is the time to feel triumph, and yet, surprisingly, there is none.

'Well, Elaine,' Hans Gelderhol said gently, 'I did warn you it would be a bumpy ride.'

'Yes,' I admitted, 'it has been.'

'And I did say that there would be bruises, and damaged dreams, and frustrations along the way.'

'Yes,' I said, 'and you were right, there were.'

'But you have done more than I ever hoped for you,' he said, 'you went out alone and you found your job, and your sponsor, and your event horse, and now you have a place in the Junior Olympic Team.'

'Yes,' I agreed, 'I've done all that.' I could hardly believe it – yet it was true.

'And now you will go on and learn more, and in two years, or three, or perhaps four, it might be Elaine Elliot, instead of Hans Gelderhol, who is European Champion. I am now forty years of age,' he told me, 'I can't go on for very much longer.'

Forty! It couldn't be true, but looking more closely I saw the fine lines around the famous hazel eyes, and the grey hairs amongst the blond, and I realized that he was not the golden boy of eventing any longer.

'It would be ironic, would it not,' he said with a wry smile, 'for you to be the one?'

'It would,' I said, 'but it might not happen.' My eyes strayed to the window, and to where in the distance a little group of people walked beside a bay horse wearing a sweat rug, his head lowered, his tail swinging gently about his hocks.

'Might not happen?' exclaimed Hans Gelderhol. 'Might not *happen*? What does this mean? Does it mean that you have lost your spark, does it mean that you are no longer the girl I remember, the blue-eyed girl with the blonde hair and the slight build, not strong enough and not wealthy enough for eventing, but who burned with ambition and spurned my offer of a job, of help, because she wanted to prove she could do it on her own? What do you mean, *might not happen*?'

'I'm not sure that I know myself,' I said, 'but I do know that situations change, and people change, and ambitions change with them. I *was* determined to succeed, I wanted to show you I could do it, I wanted your admiration. I wanted success, too, and fame perhaps, and love, I wanted that most of all, but I didn't know it, and it seems to me that until these things are within your grasp you can't evaluate them, you don't know their true worth until you get close enough and then you find out a lot of unexpected things, and oh, I'm not explaining this very well,' I told him, 'but I've found something that might be more important than all of it. Look,' I leaned over the table and I pointed to the bay horse and even from so far away I caught a flash of purple tights and I saw that Henrietta had an arm around Legend's neck and that her head was beside his head. 'Do you see my horse,' I asked him, 'and the people with him, just turning into the stabling?'

He nodded, squinting intently in the direction of my finger; he was a little short-sighted now, the golden boy of eventing.

'Well,' I said proudly, 'that's my family.'